2 ⬛0⬛1⬛3⬛ ⬛ A⬛ 01 ⬛01⬛01 ⬛ INTER-0⬛0I FIGHT

Ketamine Rush

by Jim Marcus

December 2024

This book is set in Lato Regular 9/13
Titles in Lato Heavy 16/20

Cover:
Time Rat

by Jim Marcus 2024

Edited by Ilker Yücel

ISBN 979-8-9917282-5-6

WARNING

This book glamorizes sex, drugs, music, time travel, and a number of other parts of the human experience that may be dangerous in large quantities or if performed incautiously.

12:3: 1: 9: 18 : 4:
■ II PULSEBLACK II

"Kindness eases change

Love quiets fear..."

-Octavia Butler

Chapter One:

The Convention.

Six Times

That's how many times I've been here, I've been told. And I still haven't run into myself. Which makes me wonder if all I ever did here was get railed behind a fusion taco stand. If so, I'm good with it.

I hope it was as good as this time, with this guy.

"Hey, what is your name?"

"Are you going to yell it out or something?" he deflected.

"What do I look like, some internet porn star?" I would have yelled it out like a fucking top-of-the-line internet porn star.

He didn't stop. I was leaning against the metal grill of the back of Tito's Time Munchers French Mexican Taco Cafe while he fucked me from behind. My jeans had been pushed down to my ankles and his were off completely, lying in the dirt. I understood now that this meant that he could take off running at any moment while my first few steps would probably include a half-naked faceplant. He was smart, apparently, something I had missed earlier. He was blonde, making it easier to miss that. He had nice cheekbones. His hair was a little wet, like he'd been in the rain. It made him look rugged and wild.

I want to say his name was Alan.

"It's Albio. It's a hard name to forget, " he whined.

I instantly forgot it and asked whiney to choke me.

"Coming up," he spit out, cumming and choking simultaneously.

"Fuck. Kerys, I'm cumming," he bragged, knowing my name.

I met Albio in the "Ancient artifacts of time travel" section where you could see all the shit that stupid time travelers had left behind in the past, probably when they died doing something stupid. At a certain point, time travelers became pretty much the natural diet of dinosaurs and prehistoric Giant Blood Worms™.

Little known fact: since Giant Blood Worms™ had no skeletons and were just massive, vicious ambling floppy bags of man-eating ravenous blood, snot, and mucus, scientists had no clue that they dominated nearly completely the entire planet up until about one hundred million years ago when it got too cold for them and they peaced out forever.

No bones, no fossils.

So, that's how Giant Blood Worms™ got left out of the story of world history until the invention of time travel allowed us to meet them and feed them a steady supply of yummy stupid time travelers. This is mostly how we discovered that dinosaurs had feathers and were just, basically, giant ducks, filling the warm oxygen deprived Triassic, Jurassic, and Cretaceous Period air with massive earth-shaking quacks.

Stupid time travelers.

Who are known, by the way, euphemistically, as "Rats" for reasons to come later.

I was one, Albio was one, everyone here at the time traveler's convention was one. We were just all from different times. Rats from various different sinking ships.

It wasn't mandatory and it wasn't forbidden. Most people in charge just looked the other way and let unmitigated capitalism take over, which, by the way, describes nearly every other facet of human interaction throughout history, too.

As long as we all agreed to have our memories wiped when leaving the convention, no one much cared. And if you met yourself from a previous visit, usually you just hung out a bit. depending on your self-esteem, really. Do you like yourself? That's a question you find out the answer to pretty quickly when you run into a version of you from last year who wants to just hang out and talk and find out if that little condition cleared up or if you need cream.

I mention that because as we were stepping out from behind the Taco Cafe hiding no embarrassment whatsoever, we saw three versions of the same dark haired girl hanging out sharing a milkshake. It was adorable, but if you thought too hard about it, it made your brain hurt. This girl was a younger white girl so I'm going to call her Oprah.

If you are a linear person, you probably think, "hey, I can understand how the third version of Oprah might have shown up, seen two of them drinking that milkshake and said 'can I get in on this shit' but at some point, there was only one version of Oprah hogging the milkshake. So why would I never see that version?"

If I were a high school temporal studies teacher, which I'm not because the pay sucks and your students usually, at one point, retcon you out of existence as a joke, I would say that every time Oprah moved into the realtime of the convention space, she pushed the entire place into her own objective future and overwrote the past that she jumped over.

That means that the version of this convention where Oprah had to pay for a whole milkshake on her own didn't exist anymore and, here's the hard part, NEVER existed in this timeline.

This requires us to play some kind of cruel "You're not real" games with Rats, and various bystanders, and unloved temporal studies teachers who've been retconned away by malicious grade humping Time Travelers in training.

I looked at the handsome blonde man next to me and tried again,

"Ok, one more time with your name."

"Your name is Kerys and you're from the twenty sixth century, you don't drive, and you love Asian food."

"I know MY name, showoff." I replied back to - I want to say - Aldo

"I just want to show you I was listening to YOU." He looked really cute and self-righteous, like a baby banging on the table trying to make a point to a grownup who only spoke English and not that baby shit that babies talk.

"And I was giving you my precious womanhood without holding anything back," I retorted masterfully.

"It's Albio," he laughed, unintentionally besmirching the preciousness of my womanhood.

"I don't know who names their kids that, Aldo, but it's weird." He was honestly growing on me. I don't know if I had fun at this convention before, but I sure was this time.

"Ooh, do you want a French onion bouef taco before we go to the _____ section"

"No one wants a French onion bouef taco, ever, so that's a fail, but section what?"

The truth is I wasn't listening great. But that missing word would come back to haunt me. It's apparently become important. At the time, I figured nothing I did, heard, said, or fucked would be important because my memories would be wiped when I left.

This is how it works. The convention is big. I mean, if you think about it, it gets bigger every year, right? It runs for a week of looped time. And the people in it, really, technically, never leave. It's a sustained loop. So, when I go next year, provided I'm going to, I'm just adding a person to the event.

In the center is the Rotunda, where people arrive and leave. You show up under your own volition, but you leave via the snapback cylinder. It reads your temporal signature and sends you right back where you came from, removing all memory of the specifics of the event.

You're left with an emotional awareness that you had some fun or didn't have some fun or were partially eaten by a Giant Blood Worm™ or whatever.

"What I really want is another one of these." It may give you some insight into the sensibilities of the organizers of this event to know that the highly alcoholic fruity drink things were served in a big plastic cup that had a picture of the souped up DeLorean from Back to the Future on it. I say this as a guy dressed like the terminator walks by. At least I think it's a costume. I thought I saw someone who looked exactly like me from behind, naked from the waist down, with another naked girl in just a time vest and boots. I wondered what that movie was about. I need to see more time travel movies.

I may be the only one here not all in on the classic time travel trope vintage nostalgia train.

I grab Alton's hand and drag him to the Ron Mallett Display. This is my jam. I realize, too, that this might be a good place to start. Because some people here may not understand how time travel actually works.

So let me explain. I'll start at the beginning. With dildos.

So, let's say you have the idea of a dildo. I have an idea of one myself, but it might be different than yours. But let's move past your puny dildo idea.

In order for that dildo to have EXISTENCE, to exist in our world it must PENETRATE the world.

In so many words.

It can do that by having length. That's pretty much the cost of entry for a dildo, by the way, a little bit of length. Not too much, internal organs have feelings, too. But enough to exist in the world. One dimensionally.

It also needs to have width. We call this, in the time travel community "Girth."

We don't, actually, but we should.

Most people in the know will tell you that this is probably even more important than length. YMMV.

It needs to have some height. I won't say that the person it's attached to needs to have height, because I've known some tiny little things that could peg like crazy. This is about the object itself. Length, width, height. In order for it to exist in a universe that recognizes objects, it has to have those things.

But the universe that is recognizing objects endures. It doesn't start and stop at a single point. If it did, it would be a singularity, and the software of the universe hates singularities.

More on that later.

So, it has persistence. In order for YOU to see that dildo, it has to have persistence as well. Long enough to see it, wide enough to see it, tall enough to see it and present in the right period in time to see it.

So, four dimensions. That's all it takes to be a real thing and not just the idea of a thing. For the most part.

Before, though, that dildo was a real thing in the universe, it was an idea. And one of the qualities of ideas is that they are infinitely malleable. They can be formed and shaped really easily. You can conjure one up, change it, etc. See, I just did it there with just a few words. Ideas are very friendly to change. They're like that boyfriend you had in third grade who just said yes to shit because he didn't have any other alternate opinions.

Things, however, are less friendly to change. It's almost like once you turned an idea into a thing you "baked the cake" and now changing the flavor of the cake is going to be much harder.

But not impossible. Even things that are not friendly to change can be changed.

The dildo's first three universal properties, length, width, height, assuming it's just rubber, can all be changed with an easy bake oven.

Just bake that shit, stretch it, compact it, you can make very serious changes to satisfy even the craziest and most demanding of orifices.

Even elements of the fourth universal property can be changed without too much effort. I can destroy the dildo, which, as an aside, was my favorite punk band when I was a kid, "Destroy the Dildo," and impact its duration. It stops enduring.

It stops penetrating the universe.

If I leave the dildo alone completely, which I've been known to do on occasion for weeks at a time sometimes, it will painlessly and easily time travel into the future, one day at a time, along with everything else we see. The universe has a built in subroutine for moving contiguously into the future in a steady reasonable drama-free way.

But shifting a portion of that persistence, which, for the sake of argument we can call a personal timeline, to another time that is not temporally contiguous, however, is a feat that the universe did not anticipate and will not support without violating the standard manufacturer's warranty of the dildo.

In fact, you can stop the end of that timeline at a moment where your own timeline intersects with the dildo, as we said, by destroying it. But that is literally the only method for impacting the persistence of the object that the software of the universe permits.

So, if we want to do that we have to come up with our own way.

Adolph and I showed up at the display as it started to get a little dark. I think. My memory may be a little weak, and that, in itself, is all of my problem, really. But we had stopped off for a quickie behind the Hot Tub Time Machine Full of Hard Ice Cream Soda Shop and then talked to the John Cusack impersonators for a bit.

10/10, believed them all. Even High Fidelity John Cusack. I think one or two of them may have been John Cusack.

As I dragged him, I realized that he was less enthusiastic about Ron Mallett than I was, which was a shame. I wasn't sure if he came before me or after me on the main timeline and what method he was using. It occurred to me that I didn't see his time harness. We all try not to talk about stuff like this because we're generally going to forget it anyway. But all rats have a knee jerk response to temporal information we should not know.

We don't want to know it.

But you should have all the information you can get here. So, I'll tell you that my assumption was he came from a later time. Maybe even the thirtieth century. He was traveling light. He didn't seem fascinated by the science, probably all beneath him. And he didn't seem wowed by the kitschy time travel movie nostalgia, likely because he hadn't grown up on those movies, but newer ones.

One made after I was born.

It's all remedial to him, I guessed.

But not to you, so here goes.

When I say "Software of the universe," I'm actually not being flippant. It's pretty much all the universe is. In fact, universes are made of three things, usually:

Infinity. Or some factor or multiple of infinity. Just bigness, really. Don't hurt your head around it.

Rules. Hard and fast rules for how stuff needs to happen in that universe.

Flaws. Subtle and massively overwhelmingly, disturbingly mathematically infrequent flaws in number 2.

So, basically, software. Everything else IN those universes is generated by that. Don't believe me? Fine. I'll go into detail later why you should.

But why do you need to know that?

Because the following section may save your life.

At least that's what I was told when I learned all about time travel, but that has turned out to be, really, not true. Yelling universal truths at a Giant Blood Worm™ has never bought anyone one more second of life, but you are welcome to try it.

It's necessary, because while I sit here, awash in memories of smashing a cute blonde guy over and over again, you have to sit here in school for a few more minutes so you will understand any of what's about to happen.

And school goes like this:

Top five ways to Time Travel that the Universe wants you not to do

1. Time travel via intense hard-to-achieve speed.

Einstein's theory of relativity, a party stopper for real, says that when you travel close to lightspeed, time slows down for you in a relative way. And the faster you go, approaching light speed, the slower your own timeline becomes. That time dilation can be very severe. For a proton, for example, in a supercollider that has been sped up to 99.99% or so of the speed of light, we might experience a second, but that proton is experiencing, in that same time, 27,777,778 seconds, or about 11 months. If you are a thing with mass, though, like me, approaching that speed takes more and more energy exponentially. So, even if I lost a ton of weight tomorrow, it would still take the relative energy output of many solar systems to get me near light speed.

So, what's the point of dieting? No clue.

2. Time travel via copious unreasonable amounts of gravity.

Another product of Einstein's wacky brain was the understanding that the more intense the gravity well you are in, the slower time moves. So, build a giant gravity well, like, for example, the event horizon of a black hole, and you can sort of "wait out" time and appear far in the future.

Listeners less drunk than I will likely realize that these two methods really just sort of sped up the universe's primary method of forward contiguous movement dramatically to make it look cool. If you call it what it really is, which is "alternate methods of suspended animation," it starts to sound boring again. And I'm not here to bore you. So.

3. Time travel using tiny little holes in the universe

I had mentioned earlier that universes had precise, tight-ass laws, and then, every once in a great magically numerically improbably long time, a flaw happened. One of those rules is that the space right next to this space is only one spatial unit away. This seems tautologically true, even. It's like saying that the next sequential integer is one integer away. That seems so true that even a universe with epically improbable, insanely rare flaws couldn't fuck it up.

So, you know, it does. So, sometimes these things called wormholes happen.

A wormhole is nature's way of saying, "Hey, that tiny unit of space you thought was right next to you? Well, it is, but it's also over there." What can be cool about that is that moving through time and moving through space can be the same thing, at sufficient speeds and in specific ways.

4. Time travel using tiny incredibly powerful explosions.

This is such a terrible idea that I don't want to go into it. If your goal is to travel to lots of tiny locations at the same time in little, microscopic bloody pieces, this is the option for you. Otherwise, we should move on to my favorite...

5. Time travel using swirly fucking light

This is where Ron Mallett comes in. He was a twenty-first century physicist whose father died when he was young, unexpectedly. If they had known about his hidden heart issue, they could have saved his life. Not being one of those kids who wished his father dead all day, he spent his life trying to build a time machine to do just that: warn him. The idea was that the other dimensions were malleable under certain conditions - why not the fourth one?

Adonis chimed in, "Right. That makes sense."

I jumped, "Jesus, Andy, I didn't realize you were listening."

He chuckled. "I was just agreeing. You really like this Ron Mallett guy?"

"He's the dad bod non-abusive father of modern time travel."

"Ok, so he wants to go back and save his dad. How?"

"I'm glad you asked, Artichoke." I had given up on real names at that point. How many men's names start with an "A"? It turns out at least one more than I thought.

"He used Light. The idea was that If gravity can affect time, and light can create gravity, then light can affect time"

"Definitely."

"So, he's like, we can use light to swirl around space, which, if you are on board with Einstein, is actually spacetime. You create a cylinder that holds spacetime and you swirl it with light. Then, anything you toss in the cylinder…"

"Like a dildo."

I smacked him. He had been listening. So nice.

"Can move around in the new connections made when spacetime bends a bit."

"So, you need a big cylinder? And you swirl it around like a food processor?"

"Nice." I feel like he was getting on board the nostalgia train. "Exactly."

"But we don't use a big cylinder."

"No. We flip it around. We stir it up from the inside, more like a tightly controlled spacetime tornado. "

"And now we have this."

In front of the Ron Mallett display was a new attraction. It had little holographic versions of Ron Mallett that popped up everywhere and you had to bop them on the head with a rubber Ron Mallett and earn tickets. With the tickets you could win a Star Trek: The Voyage Home whale doll or a Dr Zaus planet of the apes plushie and stuff like that.

It looked like crass commercialism, but I wanted one pretty badly for home.

I grabbed a Ron Mallett and Blondie called out the shots. We won a Quantum Leap t-shirt and then went behind the Donnie Darko Bunnie Dogs and fucked my face while I wore it proudly on my knees in the mud. It was one of those super soft shirts that felt like it had been worn already. Like my mouth. Ha. No one doubted my dedication to Sparkle Motion that day.

This was my first weekend off in months, and just saying "yes" to everything was a huge amount of fun. So, if I sound like a total whore, let me qualify that. Yes, I am a total whore, but I don't always act that way. I have been known to close my legs on occasion.

I admit I kind of liked this guy, and yes, I knew his name was Albio. It's just that's a stupid ass name and I was kind of hoping I might land on something he liked better. If that sounds manipulative to you, trying to get some guy to change his name with a preponderance of good pussy, I say fuck off, judgy. I don't tell you how to run your weekends.

I may have told him to fuck my facehole with his stupid pink horse prick super loudly in front of some people dressed like Back to the Future era Michael J Fox, but I should remind you that no one brings actual children to a time travelers' convention. If they want to look like children, that's on them.

We ate dinner at a place that had an endless X-men days of future Pasta Bar, and at that point I was feeling kind of bad that I had to leave. I have my memory wiped once when I had to trudge through about a mile of Dinosaur shit to stop a world - ending hurricane, but that was voluntary. That thirty-four minutes needed to die and I'm glad it's gone. But I honestly enjoyed this. I liked spending time with him, I liked the Kitsch, I liked it all. It was just a silly, stupid day that I thought I could use a few more of in my life.

He kissed my hand with his butter garlic lips and I liked it.

"I wish I didn't have to go." Which was actually the truth. "Will you walk me to the Rotunda?"

"It's ok," he got up. "I have to stay a little bit. You know where I'm going, right?"

I nodded. I had no idea. But this was one of those listening tests that people did all the time when they knew you didn't pay attention to a fucking word they said.

"Yep, walk with me. I can't walk straight anymore, you fucking donkey."

"Uh. A little louder, please."

I stopped Sarah Connor walking next to us and said, "This guy has premium dick."

She continued to walk, reinforcing how fucking dour all Sarah Connors are, in every timeline.

"C'mon, blondie, walk me out."

We walked past hundreds of people. It's weird what you don't take in when you think you won't remember anything. I just let it all wash over me. But I'm positive I saw a guy making out with himself and four versions of the same girl building a piece of art in the area around the Rotunda as I walked past holding hands with him holding that dumb t-shirt in the other hand.

I saw a flash, like a camera.

And then, another guy, all lit up like a blue clown, walked up to me and handed me his card. I casually took it. Laughing, he put his nose into my other hand. Clowns rock. We moved closer to the center of the place, which was packed.

Albio lifted me onto the Rotunda and kissed me for a long time. He had his hand on the back of my harness, and I wished I weren't wearing it. I wished we'd had one more chance to violate this place before I had to go. He came up for air and slid the shirt back over my head. I laughed. Ready to Quantum Leap away.

And I backed up into the front of the snapback chamber. It was time to go.

I looked at the card in my hand. It said "Inhale."

Almost without thinking, I did.

I looked up and saw Albio. He was holding my battery in his left hand. In his right hand was a gun.

There was a flash of light and I fell backward into the snapback chamber.

And everything disappeared.

KETAMINE RUSH

Chapter Two:

The Advanced Mechanics of Time Travel

Light is crazy and it's not because it's light. The universe doesn't give half a wet pigeon shit if you are a photon, which photons would know if they had any sense of perspective. The speed of light is really the speed of things that don't have any mass. Take away something's mass and it travels at the speed of light, because it can't help it. That's what the universe does with massless things. It's crazy.

So, let's say you are a photon. You have no mass. You live in a universe that seems, to you, to have no time. All your time is the same. The moment you are born and the moment you die are the same moment.

College goes by superfast.

And you can't conceive of anything moving slowly. You have one speed. 186,000 mps. The only reason this is called the speed of light and not the speed of gravity or the atomic speed is that the photon was discovered before the graviton or the gluon.

You may need this information later, so I'm sort of front loading that shit, even though it does nothing to explain how I ended up naked in an above ground swimming pool being poked with sticks by two hippies.

In the physical world, you are probably familiar with the Compton wavelength, although you might not know what it's called. This scales at $1/m$, and basically says the more massive a particle is, the less it deviates from its position at rest. So, the bigger "m" is, the smaller the deviation.

You can call movement in a space "flutter" if you want.

Do it.

This is the less common sensical version of the idea that heavy things are hard to move. When you think about photons, you end up having to consider the other side of that story. Less heavy things are hard to keep still. Photons, having no mass, have no rest state.

They flutter at infinity.

It's like the most intense version of ADHD imaginable.

Photons, and other massless particles, have no edges or surfaces. These quanta don't have length, girth, or height.

So, waitaminute, you say. How do they exist in the universe? They are clearly not like dildos.

And that is my lecture for today. Photons are not like dildos. Thank you for coming.

There may be more.

It is, apparently, enough for a particle to have energy to have a meaningful existence in our universe. Raise a little family, get a job, etc. That doesn't seem fair.

If you have energy, you can trade it for dimensionality?

Photons are like, "Yeah, bitch, we can."

It turns out that energy and mass are different forms of the same phenomena.

The energy of massless particles acts like ripples on a quantum field. And there's that word. Quantum. We're used to thinking of it as a description of how extremely small objects behave. When you have no dimensionality, you can behave like you are extremely small, because you are. You can be a particle. But you can also be a wave.

This is how the universe gets bipolar.

First of all, before I go on, I'm alive, clearly. I don't have the patience to tell ghost stories.

The hippies are wondering why there is a dead black girl in their pool, but not too hard because, besides the squirrel floating a few feet away, there are about thirty other dead things in that pool. If you own an above ground pool and you do not want to let that drag you down into abject white trashhood, it is important that you clean the fucking thing every once in a while. Otherwise, it is just a giant disease-laden petri dish in your back yard, and one day, yes, you will almost certainly find a dead naked black girl in it or start a sweeping nationwide plague or something.

Secondly, I am not destined to die in a stupid fucking above ground pool. That's ridiculous. Ask anybody who knows me.

Thirdly, even though I was face down, I had inhaled and that caused me to instinctively hold my breath. So, no offense to all you coulrophobes out there, but I will always love me a good clown.

Now, I am NOT massless or indeed very very tiny. At 125 pounds, I am probably my perfect weight, and I still own a pair of jeans from senior year of high school that fit me like a fucking glove, so don't take that to mean I'm big or anything. I'm just not one of the small things in the universe.

The rules for the universe get a little wacky for the small things. You can be a particle or a wave. Technically, at the same time. So, what is a wave?

Remember that software of the universe? It's real. One of the things it does, one of its ongoing rules is to keep track of where things are. Like keeping track of where one unit of space is, for example. It does that through continuity of connection.

Imagine you are a kindergarten teacher. I don't know why you took that job because you don't have the temperament for it, but that's not the point. We all need money to live. The point is that you have twenty demon children to teach and watch. And let's say they are out of control today.

So you go to the park.

And you say, "Ok, kids. I need you all to hold hands in a big chain, like normal functioning non water brained human children for ten fucking minutes so we can get to the swing sets, Capice?" And you watch them hold hands.

These are like the particles in the universe. You, as the "software," can sort of "feel" little Stephen at the end of that chain because he passes information to Hilde, who passes information to Monique, who passes information to the next kid, and so on. They are all particles - all kids are in a definite place, accounted for. You still have a job and are not on the registry. It's a good day.

Now.

Monique lets go. The contiguous passage of information is broken. You, as a good piece of software, know exactly when that connection was severed. And you know about how fast Hilde and Stephen can go. So now, because you don't know where they are, you have to build a probability map of where they might be. It is a circle that widens for every moment they do not deliver information to you (or a sphere if they have been known to fly or jump super high.)

That map, that area, is a probability wave. This is how Hilde and Stephen go from being a particle to being a wave. Now, once they hold hands again with Monique, once the software "notices" them in their particular form again, the probability wave collapses.

We like to pretend that it's human observation that collapses the probability wave. It's not. It's the observation from the software of the universe, and that software uses contiguous passage of information to model how it sees a particulate instance. We humans just have to be one part of that.

The main reason why this wave state happens for very tiny things is that it's a lot easier for a tiny little thing to stop, for a moment, passing information to the universe than it is for something big. It's easier for an ant to walk across your floor unnoticed than an elephant.

The hippies were arguing over whether it was racist to mention that the dead pool girl was black when calling the police with the smaller, Latin hippie affirming that it was not, in fact, racist. You see, I mentioned his race and it did not come off as racist.

Just trying to make a point.

I lifted my head from the brackish water and took a deep breath. It was sunny and warm. Surprisingly, the scent of lavender blossoms overpowered the dead squirrel scent you might have expected to dominate the space completely. A red rubber ball sat at eye level, enjoying the company of a lot of other junk.

Was that a clown nose?

I pulled myself out of the pool and flopped on the ground. I smelled the grass. I was doing a lot of smelling. It smelled like a combination of creeping red fescue and kentucky bluegrass, putting me somewhere in the American Midwest in the early twenty-first century.

There was also a billboard over my head that said "Illinois votes in 2024." But the grass thing is real. You'd be surprised how much you can tell from the grass in America.

At that moment, a friendly looking girl with a crazy afro and freckles stepped out of the back door facing the pool and handed me a towel.

"She's not dead, guys."

She looked at me as though we were the only two black women in town, and I had just shown up in a hatchback sedan from a long drive across middle America to visit.

"Do you want a hotdog?"

Her name is Davi, which is short for Davina, and she seems close to my size.

I mention this because about twenty minutes later I was sitting at the table with her, eating a hot dog, wearing a pair of her shorts and a tank top. Everything she owned seemed flowy and light and sort of wavy. Her closet was like the Stevie Nicks pure pastel collection from some slightly more bohemian version of Free People. The shorts and top were the least nonsensical thing in the place.

"You seem pretty far from home," Davi started.

"You are a fucking genius," I kicked back. That might have been unfair. But, really, did I look like I belonged here? I also felt like shit. My muscles hurt and I was waterlogged. My hands were raisin mittens.

I figured I would try the whole honesty thing.

"I'm from about five hundred years in the future. I'm a time traveler."

There was a pause at the table. I couldn't tell which direction this would go in.

The smaller of the hippies spoke up. His name may have been Sean.

"That's cool. Is everyone naked then? because that would be sweet."

"It's like liberating, right," said the other one, whose name was apparently Los.

"Nope," I continued. "It was just me. I got thrown back here without a functioning harness, which would have kept all my clothing and effects from deteriorating in transit."

Davi cut in, "I found this. Is this yours?" It was a rag that looked like it had been dragged behind a semi across two states.

"Damn. My Quantum Leap t-shirt."

"Sentimental value?" she asked.

I snorted. "Not anymore."

Sean was apparently Davi's partner. This I intuited through my keen and almost instantaneous ability to recognize social cues. They also wore matching rings and kissed a lot.

"So how do you get back?"

I looked at him like someone might look at a peanut butter and broccoli sandwich. "I don't. No part of my time vest survived. It's only a testament to the timelessness and pure watchability of Scott Bakula's sardonic performance that this even survived a little."

Los chimed in, "Can you build a new one?"

I'd been thinking about that for the last hour or so, actually. I could. I mean, I'm a physicist trained in temporal science.

But...

"Not without a UN grant. I don't mean to be classist here, but it costs a literal fortune to shove someone up time's ass."

I finished the first hotdog and moved on to the second. I tried to forget the pasta bar that was now in my past. Davi slid over a napkin.

"And no one is working on time travel right now? In this time?"

"Actually, the guy who invented it is alive right now, but no one's trying to give him any money either."

The general middling consensus around the table was that this was typical capitalism. I would have disagreed if I had any foundation to. I didn't.

That's when we heard the siren and saw the blue lights.

"Oh. Fuck. I forgot I called the police."

I thought for a minute how white that was.

As we walked out back, we saw three cops by the pool. So, this is what I know about cops from old tv movies. Police ride in twos in police cars.

So, what we were seeing was two cars full of cops with another officer somewhere we couldn't see. The three we could see were two male cops standing there with their hands on their gun holsters and one woman in blue addressing us directly.

"We heard that there was a naked black woman floating in the pool."

Ok, now that I heard it out loud out of a cop's mouth, I could see that it was kind of racist. It just hit my ear that way. I took the lead.

"It's all good, officers. Just a little misunderstanding."

"And you live here?"

"No. no. no. I was the girl in the pool. I'm fine, not dead."

Davi, Los, and Sean sort of Vannah White waved in my direction as if to showcase that I was, indeed, alive.

"What were you doing floating naked in the pool?"

"Swimming. Just a little. You know. Too much pasta before swimming."

Sean jumped in, "You aren't supposed to eat anything before you swim. Especially carbs."

"Did you call this in, sir?" she asked the white guy.

"Yes, but I wasn't really... reading the situation."

That's when I saw the fluttering red dots on all three of them. That seemed excessive. I assumed that there was one on me too, so, I dove at Davi, tackling her, trying to pull the other two with me behind the pool.

Here is where the only redeemable value of an above ground pool comes into play. The water in that pool is about one thousand times denser than air and can slow a bullet to zero within about eighteen inches when shot from a thirty degree angle. By aiming for us, on the ground behind the pool, from a standing height, they dispersed all the kinetic energy of the bullets fired before we could be hit.

Except Sean got hit.

And so did the pool. About seventeen holes peppered across the front of it, causing the sides of the pool to collapse, sending water spilling in the direction of the damage, pouring out under the cops feet. The three of them slipped in the new mud. The woman yelled out at us and got a dead squirrel in the face. That sort of felt Karmic and satisfying to me.

I grabbed the three of them and we crawled to the side of the house and ran. I saw a flash of light to my left and dodged, diving into the space right next to the house. We stayed close to the side, making it awkward for the cops to chase us. We weren't looking back, though.

Out the front and to the street, Davi raced ahead and pressed the button on the keychain around her neck. A vehicle resembling the scooby doo van sprang to life and we climbed in. Sean hit the back of the van with a thud.

"Ouch ouch ouch ouch."

"Let me see. Let me see." It wasn't a gunshot. This must have come from the missing cop. Davi started driving off and I looked around for a window. The only ones were up front.

I pulled off the ragged hem at the bottom of Sean's shirt and wrapped it around his arm. There was no blood, but I wanted to make sure.

I made my way to the front of the van.

"How come he's not bleeding?" Davi asked, eyes on the road.

"Ok, the wound is cauterized."

"What the fuck is that?" Los freaked

"It means that the wound has been closed up with a sufficient amount of heat to sort of melt the skin together."

"It actually doesn't feel too bad."

"What the fuck?" Los continued to freak out.

There seemed to be no one following us. It looked like we had gotten away before the cops had gotten to the front to see our departure. Davi looked at me.

"How could a bullet do that?"

"That one wasn't a bullet." I considered again the flash of light I'd seen.

Davi whispered, "Then what was it?"

I figured I'd whisper too, for the hell of it, "Some kind of laser energy weapon."

Davi whispered back, "See, I would have led with that."

"A laser gun?" Los affirmed and amplified his previously established trend of freaking out. Why change what's clearly working so well? I considered slapping him, but the world itself usually takes the lead in slapping people like this.

As I thought that, Davi turned quickly and he went careening into the side of the van. I should say stuff like this out loud so that people can see how fucking wise I am.

"I really feel ok. I got shot by a laser?"

"Yes, and what you're feeling right now is called neural energy expression euphoria or NEEE. It's when an energy weapon stimulates your nerve endings and supercharges them for a second, causing your body to have an adrenaline / serotonin response."

"It doesn't suck."

"Well, you'll crash, eventually and you now have a hole in your arm that you can run a tribal piercing through, so..."

"Cool."

"Pss." Davi was trying to get my attention to the front of the mystery machine by calling me like a cat. I guess it worked. "Is this a future thing?"

"Does your local police department use high output laser energy guns for house calls?"

"I do not think so."

"Then I think it's a future thing." I was starting to like her. She was witchy and weird, but seemed to have a good head on her shoulders.

We had slowed down by this point so as to not attract attention, and I had the chance to slide into the passenger seat and survey my surroundings.

"So, where am I exactly?"

"You are in Peoria, Illinois."

I spoke to myself, but it was out loud. I do that way too much. "And why am I in Peoria, Illinois?"

Los shot out from the back, "You like corn?"

"I do not much care for corn, but thank you." I turned to Davi, "He's super high right now, right?"

"Like a Northern Cardinal," she replied, "Which is the state bird of Illinois." She looked at me. "Just filling in the gaps."

"I appreciate it." And there were a lot of gaps.

Blondie shot me with something that was apparently a concussive weapon, pushing me back into the snapback chamber without my battery harness. Still, I should have ended up where I came from, which was my apartment in Norico in 2540. The snapback chamber sends you back to where your temporal signature says you came from.

I did not come from here.

The convention was sort of a vacation for me in the middle of a bigger mission. I felt like spreading everything out on a table and trying to figure out how all of this fit.

"So, what is the date?"

Los was really high. "Who the fuck knows."

Davi responded, "September 20th, 2024. Does that bring back any memories?"

It didn't.

"No. nothing. Damn."

"So, you ended up here accidentally. Where were you SUPPOSED to go next?"

"That is actually classified."

"Ok, but that means we can't help you."

I looked around the van. Los was trying to see his hand through the hole in Sean's arm, and the two of them were laughing every time the van hit a bump and they jostled and hit their heads.

"I'm ok with that."

"All right, are you in any danger? Are we? Those cops had something going on, right? It's not just about the call."

She was right. This wasn't just about swimming while black. Something was happening here. The police had information I did not, and that just rubbed me the wrong way. And energy weapons.

"We need to make some lasers."

Sean leaned in, kissing Davi on the shoulder. "That is so cool. I want a laser."

"I'll take a laser…" Los was lying on the seat in the back right now, staring up.

Davi scrunched her face up. "Can you make laser guns?"

I looked over. "Sure. I'm a twenty-sixth century physicist. I can do a lot of shit."

I was looking out ahead of me and it seemed Los was high as fuck, but not wrong. As far as I could see, there was corn. I had forgotten that corn was the dominant market produce in this time and had just not expected to see so much of it.

The good news was there were no cops in sight.

The bad news happened in a split second, it seemed. For a moment, the sky went completely dark and then everything exploded. When I say we stopped, I don't want it to sound like we slowed down and came to a stop. We were moving one second and completely stationary the next.

The windshield shattered and I went flying out of it, and penetrating the giant wet slab of meat sitting now on the hood of the van like a hot finger through room temperature butter.

Davi pulled me out by my shoulders from the other side. Apparently, I had almost gone completely through the slab of beef on the hood that was, clearly, at one point, a full grown cow.

She laid me down on the ground next to Sean and Los who were staring up at the sky intently, giggling intermittently. Then she flopped down next to me.

"You don't have seat belts in the twenty-sixth century?" I feel like it was less of a question than a taunt.

I experimented with talking. My voice seemed a bit squeaky to me, not gonna lie. "Inertial Dampeners. Hey. Let me ask you a question, Davina. Did you hit a cow?"

The guys were laughing, but still standing watch. Or I should say lying watch, investigating the skies.

Davi seemed unaffected." A cow actually hit us. It fell on us. From the sky"

I paused for a minute to take that in.

"Hey, so, historically, is that the kind of thing that happens here, during this time? Because it's, like, super rare in my time."

Everyone was staring up intently, looking for signs of future falling livestock incidents. This gave me the peace of mind to close my eyes for a second.

Sean answered, "It's some weird shit, honestly."

Davi nodded.

We all breathed in and out for an appropriate amount of time, given the situation.

Davi spoke up.

"You should probably talk to us about your job and what you're doing here. Is it connected to cows? It's about cows, right?"

I thought for longer than I needed to. "In no reasonable way I can imagine, lying on the ground right now, is anything I do even remotely connected to cows."

Sean was satisfied with that answer. "Well, I'm satisfied."

Davi seemed to want more. "If you were in this time period for work, what WOULD you be doing? Is there anything you CAN tell us?"

I considered what I could say. And how to say it. It might give me the chance to think out loud a bit.

"Well, I wouldn't be here, exactly. I would be about eight hundred miles away in Washington, DC and about fifty years from now."

Los was awake, apparently. "ooh, what happens in fifty years?"

"A very bad man with his very bad friends does something really bad. And unexpectedly bad things happen because of it."

Davi turned her head toward me. "I'm glad you opted for the really in-depth explanation."

Sean was satisfied with that answer. "Well, I'm satisfied."

I turned to Davi, "Look, I like you fucking weirdos. I don't want to make my asinine issues into your asinine issues. Originally, I thought this was just about a bad one... day... stand, but now I'm thinking it's worse than that. More serious."

"I think we're in it. At this point, you can just tell us before a whale drops on us."

Los heard that, "noooooooooooo." I had noticed earlier that among his bling was a "save the whales" patch. Sean calmed him down.

"The very bad man's name is Mitchel Wagner. He's the only reason I could possibly be here."

"Oh, " Sean responded. "You should have just said something. The Wagners live about four miles back that way."

Sean had rolled over so that he could point in the direction we had just come from.

KETAMINE RUSH

Chapter Three :

Ethical Issues of Time Travel

Two things occurred to me when walking down the road back toward the exact fucking place we had just come from on the exact fucking road we had driven on. The first was that we were right out in the open and therefore sitting dinosaurs for cops with laser guns looking for us.

The second was that, notwithstanding short, furious, unexpected bouts of situational unconsciousness caused by errant swimming pools and livestock, I hadn't slept in a really long time. And that corn field looked comfy as all fuck.

"You can't sleep in a corn field," Los flopped as he meandered down the road. "The giant machines come to collect the corn and they can run over you and crush you and just throw you in with the corn."

This sounded like total bullshit. "How do you live here and know so little about corn?"

"I," Los stood up straight, reciting as if from memory, "work for a call center, where I am able to leverage my unique people skills to provide positive solutions for people who may be initially dissatisfied with some aspect of their experience with Amazon."

Sean jumped in, "And I'm an artist. I don't really paint corn. I would if I saw interesting corn."

I turned to Davi and cocked my head. She laughed.

"I do online coaching and mediation for businesses." I don't know why that was surprising. None of it should have been.

"So, the Wagners have a fourteen year-old son named Mitchel?"

Sean raised his hand.

"You do not have to raise your hand to answer."

"I'm sorry, I thought this was like school. Yes, they do."

Damn. That couldn't be a coincidence, could it? Davi read my mind.

"What are the chances that the person you're observing lives right near where you were accidentally dropped?"

I sighed. It was pretty fucking low.

Los spoke up, "Hey, we're just giving up on figuring out the cow thing, right? It's like Area 51, where we just..." and he made a little movement with his hand to suggest that it was just sliding out of his brain.

"I think that's a good idea right now."

Davi stopped walking. I stopped right next to her. "Ok, I think we have a little moral dilemma here. Are we going to go with you and help you kill a fourteen year-old boy?"

"I'm not here to kill anyone." There was a very real chance I'd have to kill Mitchel Wagner at some point.

"You aren't here to observe him. And I don't think I can help you kill a young boy no matter what he does when he grows up."

"I'm not asking you to kill anyone or help to kill anyone or anything like that. I'm just trying to figure out why I'm here, and you said it yourself, it's unlikely this is a coincidence."

"Convince me he deserves to die."

"I'm not here to kill him."

"But you're going to kill him at some point, right?"

"I don't know. I'm observing."

"You say he's a bad man who does bad things that lead to some kind of apocalypse?"

"In so many words, yes. He is a shitty human being and everyone suffers because of it."

"So you're going to kill him?"

"Oh, my god, I don't know. Not today, not right now..."

"What does he do?"

"Do you really want to know?"

"I do," Sean seemed to really want to know.

"Yes."

I looked at Los. He looked behind himself then raised his hand.

"Davina. Years from now, Mitchel Wagner is a sitting senator. He and four of his school friends who are all high ranking members of the government rape a young woman who is the daughter-in-law of a foreign national. It's covered up as long as possible but, eventually, once Wagner is elected president, the story gets out and the country in question declares war on the US, which is forced to engage in asymmetrical warfare. The US uses nuclear weapons to fight back."

"What country?"

'The country doesn't exist yet."

Davi crossed her arms, "so, a country that is going to form in the next fifty years will be so powerful that the US will be the underdog."

"Yes."

She seemed unsatisfied with that answer.

"The country is called URB - the Unified Republic of Bharata." I waited for a second to see how good Davi's last history class was.

She put her head down. Apparently it was an acceptable history class.

Sean, on the other hand, "What is that? The country?"

I shrugged. Davi looked at him. "It's the country formed by the reunification of India and Pakistan."

"Today, that would be about 1.7 billion people."

Sean looked concerned, "How big is it in the future?"

I caught Davi's eye. "About 2.5 billion people."

Sean bit down on his slice of pizza, "That's a lot of fucking people."

It WAS a lot of fucking people. A massive number, I thought. Then I thought:

"Where did you get that piece of pizza?"

Sean pointed at Los. I looked over at Los who was also eating a piece of pizza.

What the fuck.

Davie tapped my arm and pointed. About sixty feet away, half hidden in the corn, was a pizza truck.

Los chimed in, "it's still warm."

Sean drove this time, while the rest of us ate. Honestly, I wasn't that hungry, but there were about thirty pizzas in the back and it seemed sinful to not just eat them. That's not even counting the garlic bread. I washed it down with a two liter of Orange Fanta. I looked down at the bottle. The ingredients swirled around on the label. There were a lot of them and they were very long.

The bottle silently mouthed,

"I am going to kill you my own damn self before anyone else has the chance to."

I nodded and drank.

Davi spoke up. "So, I need to think about this. Promise me we aren't going to just kill anyone until I process all this."

"I don't kill little kids. I have never had to do anything like that."

Sean looked back and Davi put a garlic breadstick in his mouth, "So how does this work. You change time and stop bad stuff from happening?

"Nope," I shot back. "You can't change time."

Los looked confused, which shouldn't even be a sentence. It's just who he is. "Then why do you go back in time?"

"All right. That's actually a very good question."

And it was. So I explained.

"People like me are called subtractionists. We work to go back in time and remove things that can cause catastrophic problems in the future."

Davi asked, questioningly, "but, why bother if you can't change time?"

"That is the exact right question and you won't like the answer. You can't change time, but you can convince time"

They all looked at me.

"Ok, does anyone here know how to curl?

"Like hair?" asked Los.

"No, like, the sport."

More blank looks.

"It's an Olympic sport."

Nothing.

"They do it at the Olympics."

Davi looked up, "Is this a different timeline thing?"

"Oh my god, Curling. A bunch of guys stand on the ice with brooms and brush the ice to convince this big puck to go in a certain direction."

Sean looked at me, "Ok, you're making that up."

I was now starting to think I was making it up. It was getting really hard to make analogies here.

"Ok, how about this, do you people know what a cat is?"

General assent

"Ok, you can't make a cat do anything. You have to sort of seduce it into doing something.

"With tuna?"

"Ok, yes, Sean, with tuna. Absolutely. That's how time is. As a subtractionist, I travel back in time. By doing that, I make that period of time into my personal timeline's future. Now there is no far future anymore on my personal timeline. So, anything I do makes my future into what it is. But it can't change the timeline of the time that I came from. That already happened."

"Ok, that makes sense." Davi was the sensible one in the pizza truck.

"Now, my personal timeline is a branch off of the main timeline that I came from. The past of it is still the same as the past of the time I came from, anything before the point where I went back. And just like a branch, it's still connected."

"Like a phone call," Los tried.

"Absolutely nothing like a phone call in any way. Connected like the fingers in your hand growing out of the same root. "

Los looked intense, "Got it."

"No you don't. You lose talking privileges. Put your head in the corner."

Sean and Los grumbled.

"Now, because they are connected, they do what's called trending. Timelines close enough together tend to develop similar patterns. If there is a massive hurricane that destroys a lot of stuff and I go back in time and stop it, then that hurricane doesn't happen in my future. Which is good. But it also impacts the future I come from, where now more timelines don't experience mass destruction, so the impacts of that destruction may be mitigated a bit. Does that make any sense?"

A pause.

Sean spoke first, "How is that like a cat?"

I waved my hands as if to wipe it all away. "Nevermind. Forget that. Did you guys see Terminator?"

Everyone had. This analogy had much more promise.

"Kyle Reese comes back. He makes the future that he is in now and that's good, but most timelines still have an AI uprising, so his timeline spits back more people going back in time to fix things. Each one of these people makes the future for their own timeline something better than what they came from, BUT still many of the branches are pulling this way, toward robot domination, so it keeps happening, a few different ways.

Eventually, after, like Terminator 20, what would happen would be that the number of branches where humans were able to survive would outnumber the ones where Skynet wins, and so they would sort of pull the other timelines in that direction. Eventually, most of the timelines will be better for human survival. It's like herding cats. Timelines tend to follow other timelines. It's called trending."

"Jesus, That was a painful and circuitous explanation."

"How about for ME, Davina? How about the fucking pain for ME? That was like a million little stabs in my brain, Davina. What about ME? God, you people are like the fucking worst sidekicks ever in history."

"Sidekick," Los seemed to like the idea.

Sean pulled the pizza truck over and announced, "ok."

I looked around. "Is this where the Wagners live?"

Sean looked confused. This was getting old.

"No, but...." He looked triumphant as he pointed out an old looking storefront. A white on black sign hung on the front with the words "Urban Artifacts" in all capital letters.

"If you want to replace your Quantum Leap shirt, this is the place."

We wandered into the store. As a time traveler, this should have been a fascinating experience for me.

"You know, this isn't the massively urgent enterprise you might think it is."

Sean shrugged. "Yeah, it was on the way. I might get one, too, honestly. "

I looked at him.

"I wouldn't wear it at the same time. I'm not 'that guy.'"

Davi looked like she was in heaven. There looked to be a bit of a hippie clothes section. It occurred to me I was still in a pair of shorts and a tank top.

"I actually need shoes, I think."

Davi walked up and handed me the pink converse hightops. "Size 8."

"Ok, right size, wrong universe." I could probably paint them with a marker. I do want to take a moment and remind everyone here that I'm a twenty sixth century physicist. I may be reminding you all of that a lot so I will make one of those hashtags you twenty first century geniuses love so fucking much. #26CenPhy.

Sean walked up, "Ta-da" in his hand he held the hanger for an identical Quantum Leap shirt. That seemed awfully convenient. So I mentioned it.

"That seems awfully convenient."

"Not really, there's a whole wall of 'em over here."

We walked over to the larger room and I could see what he meant. On it were rows and rows of Quantum Leap shirts, with about thirty matching the one I had lost perfectly.

"Hey, Sean, how close is this to your place?"

"It's just a few blocks, really, we're almost there."

"And are there any other collectibles stores closer?"

"Nope. If so, we woulda gone." He pronounced with finality.

Davi looked at me, "What are you thinking?"

"I have no money. And I need a shirt, shoes, and a pair of jeans."

"I got you, but seriously, you have the eyebrow thingy."

I pulled her aside. "This is going to sound crazy."

Davi rolled her eyes. It was a good point, that eye roll. It wasn't wrong. Acceptable gesture.

"There's this thing called the serendipity express. It's what happens when you go back in time and the timelines trend in a direction that is trying to get you somewhere. So, it sort of greases the wheels. You watch out for it. Whenever you find yourself saying 'Oh, that's convenient' too many times, like an abandoned pizza truck in the middle of nowhere. Or shirts exactly like the one you're looking for."

"So, be careful when the universe seems to want to help too much?"

"Exactly."

"And if the universe is trying to get in your way, say, by dropping a cow on your van, be careful of that, too?"

I nodded. "Absolutely."

"So, we're looking for, like, a happy medium where the universe doesn't really care what we're doing?"

"Wow, you pick this stuff up really well. I'm legitimately impressed. We should leave these guys here. They'll probably just think they live here."

Sean and Los were topless trying on t-shirts. Los had also removed his pants for reasons that evaded me.

He was wearing spongebob boxer shorts because of course he was.

I stared.

Davi came up behind me. "Come on."

We made our way over to the dressing rooms and she handed me the bag. The shirt felt identical to the one I'd lost and the jeans fit great. The shoes were really fucking pink. I stepped out, shoes first.

"Wow. Those are pink."

"These are like inside-of-a-vagina pink."

"They're Nazi-Triangle-on-a-gay-guy pink" Davi offered.

"They're Tried-to-commit-suicide-just-a-little-in-the-tub pink," I countered.

"They're Strawberry-Shortcake-falls-off-a-bridge pink," she finished.

"Hey. So, John, An interior designer, was designing a house for this family of salmon. So he says to the daddy salmon, 'I painted it Salmon colored, I'm sure you'll love it.' and the Daddy salmon says, 'so, John, it's beautiful iridescent gray and blue like my scales?' and John looks uncomfortable and Daddy Salmon looks at the house and says 'Why is it pink, John, Why? WHY IS IT PINK?' I shook her as hard as I could.

Someone needed to shake some sense into this bitch.

"Laugh, you cunt, This is a five hundred-year-old joke."

She laughed.

Then I saw it out of the corner of my eye.

Sonofabitch.

I started running toward the front of the store. He looked straight at me. He jumped over the counter and ran out the window.

I cut past the counter and followed. He turned left out the door and I followed him, grateful I'd actually fucking tied those pink ass shoes. He dodged into a gangway and I turned and followed. I nearly caught up to him in the gangway until it ended abruptly with a chain link fence that he launched himself over.

I was faster, but He could climb like a fucking monkey. He also knew the area better, it looked like. I let myself fall down the other side of the fence and kept running. I followed him into the alleyway and into the first yard on the right he had slid into. He was hoping to get far enough ahead that I couldn't see where he was going, but I kept gaining. Not enough fences and gates for him to scale.

I moved left, forcing him to run through the lit brightly colored firepit in someone's LGTBQ grandpa's backyard, and he lost a few feet. I gained in the gangway and then swung around to the front of the building. The fence in front of him was locked and topped with spikes, and it looked like he hadn't anticipated any of that.

I quietly thanked gay grandpa and slammed into him as hard as I could, making sure the back of his head hit the fence hard.

He flopped down in front of me.

I leaned over and put my hands on my knees. Then I picked him up and dragged him back to the van.

Davi looked him up and down. Now that he was naked, I was even more sure it was him. I poured a two liter of sprite over his head and he woke up. I pulled the pizza box tape off of his mouth.

"What the fuck?"

Sean looked concerned, "Are you sure it's him?"

I looked at the guy, naked and tied up in the back of a pizza truck and nodded. He had dark hair now, but there was no doubt in my mind it was him.

"Hello, Albio." I bet he would be surprised I remembered his name now." Truth is, I had written it on my hand.

"My name is Alan. Where are my clothes? What the fuck? What did you..."

"Shut the fuck up. You know what? YOU fucking wake up after being knocked unconscious for once. It sucks. You suck."

"I didn't do anything."

"Then why did you run?"

"Because you were chasing me?"

That wasn't a terrible point.

"You don't remember me?"

"Look, you're crazy, but you're hot. I wouldn't forget you."

Davi looked over at me, "Is there a chance it's not him?"

There was no chance. I knew it was him.

Los interjected, "He IS naked, just like you were when you showed up."

"I'm the one who made him naked, Super Mario. I took his clothes off, you tiny idiot."

"Where are my clothes?"

"Gone. You don't get to run away. I get to figure out why you shot me and sent me here."

"Whoa. I didn't shoot anyone. And you look fine."

"With a concussion pistol, you idiot."

"What the fuck is that? And what is it? Tuesday? Don't you people have fucking jobs?"

Davi pulled my shirt up.

"Do you remember these?"

"Damn. You guys really are crazy."

Davi was shaking her head, "I actually think he honestly doesn't know."

How is that even possible?

Sean took a bite of the calzone he was eating. "Hey. Could this be the guy, but BEFORE you met him?"

I looked at Davi. She shrugged.

What the fuck just happened? Was Sean paying actual attention?

Davi bent over to talk to him. "Hey, Alan. Have you ever been to a time traveler's convention?"

He looked up, panicked.

"Holy shit, you guys are really fucking nuts. Help!! Help!!" I'm being raped. Rape!!" HE started thrashing around. I kicked him and put the tape back on his mouth.

"FUUUUCK"

Davi was driving now. "Is this a good idea?" She looked over at Sean in the passenger seat, "Sweetheart. You had enough."

He smiled and put the pizza down. We had gone through a ridiculous amount of pizza and breadsticks. "Are we really raping this guy?"

"No one is raping anyone. I'm trying to figure this out." Then it hit me. The shirt.

"Holy shit."

Davi looked at me. I feel like she'd grown up a lot in the last couple of hours.

"The temporal signature of this shirt. It's from this time."

Davi shrugged.

"The snapback. It used the temporal signature of the shirt I was wearing. This doesn't just feel like that shirt. It IS that shirt."

"So the shirt is going to be at the convention later?"

I looked at her. "Maybe."

"So, maybe he won't be there until later, too. Maybe he's telling the truth."

Bless her heart. "Men don't tell the truth."

She pointed to Sean, "This one does."

Sean smiled. I swear to fucking Buddha if this fucking hippie was right I was going to eat my colon.

Los added, "So no raping anyone."

Davi and I responded, "NO."

"And here we go." Sean pulled up in front of a bungalow with a big wide backyard. I leaned over and popped open the glove compartment, grabbing a folder full of some papers. Opening the door a bit, I hopped out.

"I need you to stay here and watch him. Is that doable?"

I trotted up to the front of the house. Davi leaned out the window and yelled, "Don't kill anyone." I waved at her and continued.

I rang the doorbell. A shorter woman with a tightly curled perm came to the door.

"Hi, Mrs. Wagner?"

"Can I help you?

"Yes, I'm sorry. I'm Miss McFly, I'm the TA in Mitch's business class."

"Oh, hi, very nice to meet you. I'm Mitchel's, well, Mitch's mom, Janice."

"Well, hello, Janice. Your son was in such a hurry to get home he forgot these papers for the mock business. I was hoping I could get them to him.

"Oh, no problem. If you want, they're in the back. The boys. You can just walk around back and give them to him."

"Oh, thank you." I moved around to the side of the house. At this point, I had no real idea what the hell I was going to do, but I had nothing but questions and just one answer would help. Just one fucking thing that I could figure out that would make some sense.

I walked up to the gate and looked back. There were about fifteen boys running around, all in their boy scout uniforms, and off to the side, with a bowl cut and acne spots on his forehead was the person I'd grown to think of as the most evil person alive, Mitchel Wagner, staring right at me.

I dropped the papers and walked back to the van. It was gone. I looked up and down the street. One street down and to the right I saw the van.

The universe had finally answered the age old question, "How long can you drive an abandoned pizza truck around before the police stop you," and the answer seemed to be less than three hours. Davi, Sean, and Los were being handcuffed and put into police cars.

I didn't see Albio anywhere. Was he still in the truck? I made note of the precinct number on the back of the police car as it drove off and looked around. I backtracked a bit until I was standing almost in front of the Wagner house.

What was I hearing?

It sounded like heavy breathing.

I looked across the street. And there was a pink globe sticking out from a bush. I walked over.

"Hey. Alan."

There was a pause.

"Well, at least you believe that's my name now," He was almost completely hidden in the bush.

"I can see your butt from across the street."

"Well, spank my ass and put me on the sex offender rigistray, maw."

"Why aren't you in the truck?"

"The little guy let me go because he he didn't want you to rape me."

"No one's going to..." I sighed.

"Just answer me one question honestly. You live here, right?"

"I live like seven blocks away."

"But, here, like now, right? In this time?"

"Yeah, because I'm not insane. I don't think I'm in Twelve Monkeys or something."

"I need your help to get my new friends back."

"I need clothes, a new job, and ongoing PTSD care."

"Ok, fair enough. Let me find you some clothes." I looked in all directions and tried to get my bearings.

"Then we need to make some laser guns."

Chapter Four :
#26CenPhy

"So you don't have any money at all," Albio grilled me in the Pawn shop, which sounds way dirtier than it was.

He grilled me right in the fucking pawn shop. Oh yeah, How hard?

"I'm from the fucking 26th century."

"So they don't have any money at all in the fucking 26th century"

"No, we do. I just showed up here in this timeline ass up buck naked because of you."

"Ok, but, and hear me out, no, because I have never met you before."

"Well, I think you're going to meet a lot of me, real soon."

"Ok, that makes no sense. What are you looking for, again?"

"A dvd writer. People in your time used them to watch and burn movies filled with cartoon animals."

"I know what it is. Are we gonna bootleg some blu rays?"

"Nope. We're going to make laser guns and steal some hippies from the cops."

"I am 100% sure you should not be saying that out loud."

"Why? No one believes me anyway."

He tilted his head to one side. No defense. I rang the tiny silver bell on the counter. A puffy man with no hair or eyebrows came out from the back. He looked like a Kielbasa.

"I am looking for these things." I handed him a list. He squinted at the list and then at me. He paused for a second as though floating in a pot of hot dog water.

"Man, I used to love that show. Whatever happened to that show?" I looked down at the t-shirt and up at him.

"It got canceled. Shitty ending, too."

"I hear you," he shook his head, adjusted his mustardy bun and slid into the back, amidst a trail of chopped onions.

"He's going to get that stuff, right?"

I stared into the doorway the sausage man had disappeared into, "I don't think we're meant to know."

"You can build an energy weapon with the stuff on that list?"

"I can. #26CenPhy." I made a hand motion. I would revisit it later.

"Ok, I have no idea what you just said."

"Are you bullshitting me? Can you just tell me if you are, because this is really shitty. I actually liked you, you know that, before you shot me in the face."

"Look, I'm sorry that guy shot you in the face, but it wasn't me. I have literally never shot anyone in the face. Would I hang out in a carnival with you and fuck behind various food stands? Yes, Probably, probably I would, you're hot as shit. But, you're also crazy and I don't shoot people, even crazy ones. Especially crazy ones, actually, because who knows how that's going to go? Bad probably."

"Fuck you. I'm not crazy. I'll shoot YOU in the face."

"Now, that sounded crazy."

The Bratwurst came out with a bag from the back. "I think this is everything. Be careful with this cable, it's a bit worn, he wienered."

"That's fine." I looked at Albio.

He sighed and pulled out his debit card. I leaned over to see.

"Your name is Alan Biolensky?"

"Yes."

"And you really don't see how you might have come up with Albio?"

"Yes, I mean, I see it. It's just that no one calls me that. Ever. And I'm not blonde."

"I swear to Odin, I will fuck you up all over your face if you are shitting me."

"Oh, look. I'm paying for your shit right now. Swipe"

Normal light is incoherent. Kind of like Los. It's all over the place. You can give light coherence in two ways. One way is to spatially filter it. This is like sending it through a tiny little fucking hole. Now, it slips through and the waves are sort of aligned in a row, timed perfectly. Light has gone from multiple sources, all over, to one source, tight waves.

We can then, also, temporally filter it. We do that by sending it through a color filter. Now it's all one color. It's directed, it's monochromatic, it's coherent.

Except, by that time, it's lost a ton of its energy. DVD writers use electronic circuits to pump and turn incoherent light into directed, coherent light. It's a good start. And it keeps you from having to build about 80% of the whole thing. You just have to take apart your DVD and find a different way to watch Frozen.

Life is about sacrifice, bitch.

Now, we need a gain medium. To pump that shit up so a little coherent light becomes a lot of coherent light. We can excite a bunch of electrons that then slap the photons on the ass and say, "You go girl." And then a lens to focus it.

And now, you're ready to put a hole in someone.

He stared over my shoulder like a puppy dog for about 20 minutes first.

"I should probably tell you, I'm letting you use my garage because I'm actually attracted to you, even though I think it's a terrible idea."

"What is?"

"Being attracted to you. It's a really bad idea. I mean, I can tell immediately."

"Exactly what about me are you attracted to?" I simmered.

"Well, honestly, you're hot, you're crazy, and you're making a high impact energy weapon out of a twenty-year-old entertainment center with no bra on, so it's a little hard to figure out where to start".

"I'm wearing a shirt."

"Yeah, but every time you swear, your tits bounce up and down a bit and it's mesmerizing."

This wasn't untrue. I'd been noticing it for a couple hours myself. I bounced a little.

"Hold this."

"Is it going to explode?"

"Let's both assume I'm not trying to kill you until we get my hippies back."

"Wait, I'm going, too?"

"Why do you think I'm making two ray guns?"

"How am I supposed to tell what the fuck you're doing? I'm like a monkey over here, you're so much more advanced than me."

Now, I may need some help with this. I was barely turned on when he was telling me how hot I was and fawning all over me. But now that he's called himself a monkey, suddenly he smells amazing. What the fuck is wrong with me?

"Fuck, do you have a camera?"

"One I don't need?"

"It's time to live on the edge, monkey."

"Fine." He dug out his camera bag and handed me a Nikon, which I took apart in front of him while he stared like I was dissecting his cat.

"They have tiny mirrors I need for lensing. And, done."

They didn't look great, but I figured they'd work. I handed him one.

"Come on."

Albio lived in a tiny house with a big garage and a massive yard. It was a weird tradeoff that a horse might make if it was looking for property in upstate Illinois. There was a tree in the center of the land that looked like it had been there for generations. Fuck you, tree.

"Ok. hold it like this. Have you ever shotten a gun?"

"Yes, many timeseses"

"Well," and I smacked him in the back of the head, "forget all of that."

"You know, I probably have a concussion from you knocking me out earlier."

"Look, you're worried about your brain damage, I'm worried about your brain damage, suddenly, no one gets anything done. Now. This is a Ray gun. Cool, I know, but it has no drop and it has no kick. So don't expect any movement of the gun in your hand and don't aim high like you might do with a projectile weapon where the bullet drags due to gravity. "

"Can I hold it cool like this?" He held the gun to the side a bit like a gang member in a primarily gay Law and Order spinoff.

"No, don't invent anything. Just shoot that tree."

"Ok." He aimed and a four foot hole opened in the center of the tree as it caught fire.

He dropped the gun. "Holy fuck. You're going to fucking kill everyone."

"One second." I adjusted the spread. The hard part about lasers is not creating sufficient gain, but really, keeping the beam tight over distance.

"Kerys."

"I got it, keep your pants on."

"Kerys."

"I have to tighten the lenses."

"My house is on fire."

I looked up. The tree had tipped over, dispensing flames which had jumped in the light wind to his tiny house, now being swallowed from the roof down by a series of orange-red tendrils as black smoke billowed up from the top.

"Shit."

He wasn't talking to me for the first twenty minutes of our walk to the police station. And then he stopped, right in front of a Lowes home repair and construction megastore. We had passed like four of these and it seemed like Peoria's second big investment after corn. I'd been thinking a bit about how to diffuse this situation.

"Realistically, you were renting."

"I'm homeless ,and the only things in the world I own are this raygun and the clothes on my back."

"I left your other clothes in a backyard, I'm sure we could find them. And the gun is mine."

He looked at me and threw the gun as far as he could. It got some good air before landing on a roof. I looked up at it. That was probably going to cause some trouble down the road in this timeline.

"Great. Now we only have one. So, stay behind me."

"Why am I doing this?"

Ok, if you are reading this, you might appreciate my own breakdown on that question. I had basically kidnapped and stripped this guy, tortured him a little - virtually not at all if we're going by the established Geneva convention guidelines - then cost him his job and, super recently, burned down his house. So why WAS he still here helping me?

Top five reasons Albio was helping me:

1. Simple. His dick.

I don't want to say men are easy, but they aren't Linear Algebra. I think we established a while ago that he was attracted to me.

And I wasn't being coy. Davi flashed him my tits, and don't think I didn't enjoy stripping him naked just a tiny bit. It might sound man-hating to say that men will do anything when turned on, but it's really man-loving, if you think about it. The way to a man's heart? Start low.

2. Misplaced loyalty.

He was probably just raised in one of those weird hyper-healthy households that encouraged him to maintain loyalty to people past his own personal boundaries because people are good and you can help them. So, when the hippies let him go, he now feels some sort of weird ambient pull to save them. It's not me at all, but them. This is going to get him fucked up one day. I hope it isn't this one.

3. Stockholm Syndrome.

If you're unfamiliar with this, it's an evolutionary imperative that causes people to create a deep bond with the person who kidnaps them out of a biological drive to survive and maintain a position in the gene pool, even if that position is choiceless and not optimum. It's about breeding, deep down, and it's dirty and sick and hot, and I was hoping it was this one. He was no wealthy newspaper heiress, but he could be my bitch forever, and that could align with my needs because I hate doing laundry.

4. The Weirdness Hole.

There is a condition that was identified in the 24th century called Novelty Hypnosis. It's what happens on a time jump to a rat when your surroundings are so bizarre that they sort of suck you in and confound your brain, kind of like when a crow finds a gold watch in the street, all sparkly and moving and shit.

So you slide down the weirdness hole in abject fascination, and you often can't come back out until you intentionally shake it off. It makes you want to be close to the weird and figure it out. But you never can.

5. He's a nicer person than I am.

Do I believe this one? No. But I could just be a person in obvious trouble and he's a truly nice person who wants to help. I'm unsure if this is actually how the world works, so I leave this one last. Do with it what you will.

We arrived at the front of the police station. We ducked down below the bushes across the street. I figured Albio would be right at home.

"How do you feel about doing laundry?"

"Fuck you."

So that went like that.

And then I saw it. There were a number of cops hanging out in front of the police station. They were all dressed a little differently, some in uniform, some in plain clothes, some wearing vests, some looking like little kids playing dress up.

And that one was wearing a time vest.

"Do you see that guy?"

"Which one?"

"He's wearing a time vest and I want it."

"Well, Christmas is still like three months away, so..."

"Watch this."

"I placed the gun low to the ground and waited for traffic to stop completely. Angling the beam a tiny bit up, I targeted the gas tank of the cop car farthest from the front of the building. I quickly pulsed the gun so fast that it would have been nearly impossible for anyone to notice the flash.

The results were noticeable, though. The car blew up, sending pieces upward almost twenty feet. As I suspected, the mob of cops ran off to the car, toward the explosion, to see what had happened, while the one cop in the time vest stopped, and cautiously looked around. He started walking around the back of the building.

"Come on."

We followed him to the back. There was a door back there that led into the station. My guess is that the time displaced phonies used this door. I held up the gun.

"Stop, turn around. Don't touch anything."

He turned around. The fact that he recognized what was in my hand immediately reinforced my suspicion he was from the future. He held his hands up.

"Oh. ok. Did you tighten the lenses on that?"

I looked at Albio.

"She burned my house down."

The fake cop was red faced and thick, but calm and reasonable looking. He was sort of shaped like a strawberry, with massive shoulders and teeny tiny lower parts.

"My friend is going to get your weapon."

"We're actually not close."

"Ok. all good. We are all just talking"

Albio frisked him and pulled out a light gun and a time period appropriate projectile weapon. I spoke to him, keeping my eyes on the berry.

"Hold on to the light gun. We're going to ditch the other one."

"Tell you what. If you leave it in a dumpster in back, I'll get it later and no kids will find it, fair?"

Albio nodded. I barked, "Now give me the vest."

I expected him to run, I think. Without their vests, rats are trapped. He started taking it off.

"It doesn't work. None of them work."

"Right." I stepped closer and grabbed it. It was a little older than mine but still in good shape. There were differences, the kind you'd expect from different timelines. But it was a time vest.

"What do you mean none of them?"

"There were five of us who came here. We're just like you. Two days ago, all five of the vests stopped working."

"When are you from?"

He looked nervous. This wasn't the thing you usually talked about.

"Twenty Six Twelve."

"Nope, try again. This vest is older than mine."

"It was my dad's, originally. He was a subtractionist, too. We all are."

"What job were you on?"

Albio looked frustrated and freaked out. "We need to get out of this alleyway soon."

"He's not wrong. But I'm on the Nuclear Demon thing."

"What?" I had half expected him to be on the same job I was on. "Can we get in this way and get our friends?"

"The guy I shot earlier today, I know. Go in here and take the elevator up to five. They're still in processing."

"Ok. great. Now give him your clothes."

"How did you learn how to tie people up like that?"

"It's the primary rule of bondage. I can tie you up quickly or untie you quickly. I can't do both. How's the outfit?"

"Big in the shoulders, snug elsewhere."

"Did you see that guy was shaped like a strawberry."

"Feeling it."

We stepped out of the elevator into chaos. I had started to wonder why they hadn't been processed yet. It was becoming clear why. I put my hands behind me and Albio marched me up to the front desk. He put on his best cop face.

"Hey Sarge," he called out over the noise. "I need to put this one with her friends."

The beleaguered sergeant, a puffy-faced croissant whose badge read "Cleveland" waved him on to a door to the left of him.

Albio pulled me through the door. I whispered, "Tighter," and he shook his head. I saw Davi toward the back of the room. She sat on a bench looking down. Sean's head was in her lap and Los was lying on the floor next to them. I sat down next to her.

"What are you in for?"

"I swear to god, if you two stopped to make sweet love before getting us, I will be pissed."

"Nope. We didn't even go to the bathroom, right?"

Albio pulled the little knife out and started cutting off the ties that the police had put on everyone's wrists.

"She burned my house down."

"He was renting."

Sean sat up, "And despite it all, he became a cop, which shows that you can do anything."

"Nice vest," Davi fingered the material.

"It's so I can get out of here and stop torturing you fuckers."

Albio stood up with authority, "All right, let's go, people."

Sean and Los jumped to attention, Davi and I joined them. I looked at Albio.

"I'm still tied up."

He smiled and grabbed my arms. "Move along, convict."

Sean was impressed, "He's very good."

We stepped past the metal detector to go down the main way. Albio slipped the Colt out of his holster and put it in the bin. We kept moving.

Out in the alleyway, the strawberry was gone.

Albio was concerned. "This was too easy."

He didn't get it because he was so used to being what he was. Letting us finish up and get the hell out was the best way for the berry to keep his cover as a cop. And the cover was more important than we were.

We started walking toward the street behind the station. Albio's clothes were stashed in the alley there, so he rolled up the police uniform and slid it into the dumpster, and pulled on his own clothes,

I looked across the street.

"Hey, maybe I'm wrong, but did someone at some point say it was Tuesday?"

Across the street there was the Owl's Nest. And a sign on the front that said, "Tuesdays all you can drink well drinks 5 dollars."

Between the four of them, they had twenty-five dollars. I want to reassert that I usually pay my way, but the circumstances of my appearance in this timeline made that hard.

Sean toasted us, "To our rescuers. And the reason we were arrested in the first place."

Davi looked suspicious, "So, you two have made up?"

"I'm no longer a hostage. I was promoted to perpetrator."

They all cheered and drank.

"I think Sean was right. For Albio, I think the convention is in the future."

"And I can't imagine why I would ever want to shoot you in the face."

They cheered and drank to that.

"Well, you disabled my vest and shot me with a harmless concussive gun to send me back here. So what if that's what you needed to do to get me here? Or what you will need to do?"

"So, I wasn't - won't be - trying to hurt you. I'm just trying to get you where you need to be for... something?"

"And the shirt. You planted it so that I would end up being sent to the temporal signature start for the shirt, not for me. Disabling my vest made sure that I wouldn't leave right away. "

"I can't believe I'm asking this, because I can think of so many reasons to shoot you, but why a concussive gun? If future me wanted to send you here, why not just kick you into the machine and send you back? "

Davi asked, "Well, what does a concussive gun actually do?"

"It basically... I get it. It knocks you unconscious for a minute or two and throws you backward."

"So, you were unconscious going into the machine." Davi took a drink.

"And the snapback couldn't access my memories precisely so it left them alone."

"And that's why you remember all of it." Albio took a drink. This was like the world's shittiest drinking game.

"Ok. I was destined to come here, scope out Mitchel as a kid, meet you guys, burn this guy's house down, and what, go?"

"That's kind of a letdown," Los said. He was looking through his pockets.

Sean lifted his beer. "I think they took his drugs."

Albio looked over and drank. "Savages. That's it. I'm retiring from the force."

And everyone drank to that a lot.

Davi and Sean danced slowly to a song called "Muskrat Love" on the jukebox that Los had programmed to play about ten times. He made her laugh and he was loyal. I get it. Not my size sweater, but she seemed like she knew what she wanted.

Los was dancing with a mop he had removed from the back room and making it look harder than it should have been by all logistical considerations.

And Albio and I danced in the middle of the back room of the Owl's Nest in Upstate Illinois on a Tuesday afternoon at the beginning of the 21 st century.

"I am sorry about your house."

"You know, every few minutes, you just stop and remember something that was in there and you kind of freak out again. But then, you remember that you never liked your landlord and the toilets backed up a lot, and it's better."

"So, you're a glass half full motherfucker."

"Exactly."

"Ah, I'll miss you most of all, Piglet."

"I'll miss you, too, Eyeore."

"Really? I'm Eyeore? "

He laughed, "You're like a demonic lovechild between Eyeore and Tigger."

"I'm all Tigger, bitch."

"You may be right."

The following was technically our first kiss, but I don't want to minimize the fact that, in my personal timeline, he had his tongue up my ass about twenty-four hours ago.

"What are you thinking?" He asked.

"If we ever hang out again, you will remind yourself, in detail, why you should never ask me that."

We kissed harder. I grabbed his hand.

While I'm sure we weren't the first people to have sex in the Owl's Nest bar unisex bathroom, I have to feel like we were among the best. When I tell you we had a sinkbusting good time, I don't mean that euphemistically.

We kissed hard in the bathroom, clawing at each other's clothes. His tongue snaked down my throat as he lifted me onto the sink, spreading my legs. My jeans were on the floor this time, and I pulled one leg up on the sink next to me so he could get deeper.

I wrapped my arms around him and pulled as tightly as I could. It felt the same as it did yesterday. It felt amazing.

It felt like what I should be doing with my vagina right now.

And so I did it.

We got back to the table to see Sean and Davi looking at each other romantically and Los flopped down on the table. Still flushed, I kissed Davi hard on the lips.

"You'll always be my best bitch."

She laughed and hugged me.

I gave Sean a hug and kissed Los on the head. He needed some sleep.

I checked the battery and the fit of the vest. I dialed in my time and moved to the middle of the back room. I waved at the four of them and smiled what I hoped was my best "Thanks for the memories" smile.

And I activated the vest.

And waited.

Now, what is supposed to happen is that there is a flutter of light that then swims around you.

The area you can see through thins and dims, and then, the next time you can see, completely, you are somewhere else - somewhen else.

But not this time.

I clicked again.

Nothing.

I saw Los raise his head confused. That was a familiar sight. I looked at them.

"It doesn't work."

Los was pointing to my right. "I think it did."

I turned my head.

Immediately to my right I could see me, sitting crosslegged in a pair of sheer black panties, surrounded by a glow that shimmered and faded. The other version of me looked around and smiled.

"Very nice."

And then, other me threw up all over herself and disappeared.

Chapter Five:

Free Motor Home. As Is.

"Do you think the strawberry was telling the truth?" Albio asked as we sat up against the wall in the alley behind the Owl's Nest.

Los sprung to life and sat up. "Oh my god, you hear them, too?"

I sat back and knocked my head against the brick. I wanted to be unconscious again.

"No, and NO!"

Davi jumped in. "Is it the battery?"

"Possibly. It seems fine, but it could be."

Albio took charge, "So, you need a lab, we need a place to live, and everyone needs a way to get there."

Davi jumped up. "Wait. Follow me."

She started off down the block. Out of inertia more than anything else, we followed her.

"What is it?" I caught up to her.

"The serendipity express." She grabbed my arm. "If it's still there."

Albio scrunched his face, "What is that?"

"It's something we aren't supposed to do. But sometimes we have to."

"Well, optimistically, that describes everything we have done today, so…"

"We saw it from the police car on the way to the precinct, and there it is."

She pointed.

And about fifty feet in front of us was an RV with a sign on the side:

"Free Motor Home. As Is."

"Dude." Los was clearly impressed. It smelled like the last family to live here had just been steadily peeing as they had lunch, cleaned up, packed, and left.

Sean loved it, "This is the most Breaking Bad™ thing I've ever seen."

"This is definitely collateral evidence of at least one capital crime."

"Shut up, cop."

I thought Albio had quit the force. I smiled at him.

"I know we're not supposed to 'Ride the Serendipity Express', but this seemed too good to pass up."

She made cute little air quotes and faces, but she wasn't wrong. This was the universe bribing us to do…

To do what?

I suddenly wished I knew more about timelines and how branching worked. I tried this:

Top five things to know about how time moves, branches, etc.

1. Language affects the perception of time.

In England and other places born from English, we think of time as a timeline moving left to right, here right is the future. In Mandarin, time moves on a vertical line where the future is down. Greek languages see the expansion of time as a radiating sphere where the now is the center and the bigness of time is relative. The Sapir-Whorf Hypothesis says we can't think about things our language doesn't let us talk about. So, our talking about time impacts our thinking about time, which in turn impacts how we move through time.

2. Time movement is asymmetrical

We always see time mapped as branching from a single point and then spreading moving forward. This suggests that we are always making decisions which create tributaries in time, then spread out forward. It's like this. Imagine you are on top of a little mud hill and you pull your dick out and start peeing. Go ahead. Imagine. I'll wait. Now, when you look down, you will see the piss hit the ground and then spread out. If you stand still, it hits the ground at a point and then dribbles down, making a path. Until it runs into something, then maybe it splits. And now there are a couple of paths. And this continues until you run out of piss like the dehydrated pussy you are. It's not going to run back up the hill. And even though, every once in a great while, tributaries merge again, they mostly split more and more. If there are many tributaries that are very close together, they may create a confluence, seemingly merging back together.

This gives you a mostly unified timeline with a few disparate past events. This is an example of trending. People in the 21st century call it the Mandela effect. Forward in time is different from the other way. And the fact is the universe is constantly pushing that way.

3. Ontology and origination is not a problem for the universe.

There is a paradox called the ontological paradox, and it has to do with causation and creation. Let's say I grab a bunch of original screenplays for some David Fincher movies and put them in a box. I go back in time to give them to him. He's like "What's in the box?" but then he likes them and makes them into movies. He originally wrote them, but in this new timeline, he didn't. And that means they have no author. The movies go on to do well at the box office and many people have sex to them on Netflix. Still, no authors. And the universe says? Don't care. The universe has no concern at all. This has happened over and over again. Works of art, writing, etc. exist in various timelines that were never made in that timeline. Because...

4. All of time is one big giant ass closed system.

That's right. One big system. Energy, creation, people, things, etc. can appear in a timeline without impacting any principles of conservation or bugging any universal software concerned with the laws of thermodynamics. I could grab all of Salvador Dali's work and then go back to 1910 in Buttfuck, Spain and stab him in his little six-year-old mustachioed face, and still keep all the paintings in that timeline. The universe won't care. People don't generally do this because without a Salvador Dali, there isn't much value to "the persistence of memory," or a bunch of little gassy pictures of Lenin's face floating over a piano keyboard.

The universe doesn't care, but no one else does, either.

5. There is a "regular person" problem

The universe is brutal. No matter what you think of yourself, it wants to turn us all into regular people. Once you arrive at a point in time, your personal timeline continues on as the timeline of the universe you are in, just like everyone else. You are no different than anyone else. You may know some things, but your ability to influence anything is the same as anyone else's.

"So, I can influence time as much as you can?"

"Shit! Wait, I said that out loud?"

"Yes." Davi looked around, "You do that all the time. You just stop and make these top five lists."

"Fuck. I thought I was doing that in my head."

"So, trending is really when there are a lot of timelines that are similar and they sort of line up and pull other ones in with them."

"Yes, I just said that."

"That's a confluence." Davi asked.

"Yes."

She looked at Los. He was eating a bottle of Flintstones chewable vitamins he had found in the RV. He perked up.

"Oh, sorry. My degree is in Flow, Sediment, and Morpho-Dynamics of River Confluence in Tidal and Non-Tidal Environments."

"And you work at an Amazon call center."

"Proudly. There are forces that pull stream tributaries together and make, you know, confluences. Do you think that happens with time, too?"

"Yes. it does."

Los looked satisfied as he tried to dig out the last few Flintstones.

"And you said that all of the timelines are one big closed system. Just like how the entire waterbed would have the same water and force."

"Right."

"So, a confluence that has multiple smaller tributaries feeding into it should have more force than the tributaries- more energy, I guess? I mean if the confluence is the same general size as the tributaries. And you said all timelines are the same."

I looked up. "Holy shit. You should be able to tell if you are in a confluence."

Los poured the last of the Flintstones powder down his throat. "Yeah. More energy."

He suddenly held his stomach.

"I should go lay down."

He moved to the back of the RV. I hadn't been back there yet, so who knew what the fuck was happenning back there. Explore well, you beautiful son of a bitch.

Albio looked at me, "So, if we are in a confluence, what does that mean for you?"

"It means that I will likely show up in my own timeline if I move forward, and the stuff the universe is throwing my way is helping us to do that."

"And if not?"

"I don't know, man. It's less likely? This has a lot of catches and complexities to it. The universe sucks, to be honest, and it likes to play god. Mostly because it is god."

Davi spoke up, "Wait, we know we're in a confluence. She grabbed the Flintstone bottle. We have a Mandela effect. Some people remember this as 'Flinstones' without the 't'."

"which 't'?"

The 't' that is after the 'n'."

"Ok, assuming that's not just the product of a poor national education system, that could show one tributary or divergence. That's helpful, but it doesn't show a major confluence."

"Then you have to even find a way to make the vest work."

"Yes, I do, Albio. And that is the first fish I need to fuck up in this stupid ass clambake. So, I'm going to try to clean up the tetanus mobile and dive in. Who's with me?"

Some hands went up. Los called out from the back.

"Start back here. It's bad."

In all honesty, I needed to meditate. I didn't mean to yell. You might not be groking this yet, but I'm a pretty cool laid back chick. I'm easy going. And I'll fuck up anyone who says otherwise. I sat up front in the passenger seat. This area smelled slightly less like a hurricane of piss, but there was definitely a dead rat somewhere.

Albio sat down in the driver's seat.

"I took the sign off. This baby's all ours now."

We sat in silence for a minute. "I'm sorry the vest didn't work, but am I allowed to say I'm not sorry the vest didn't work?"

"You're allowed to say any asshole thing you want."

"I know you can't just stay here, but I..."

"Spit it out, hot fuzz."

"I am just really wishing I could see where this goes." He made a little motion pointing at both of us like I could have possibly missed his point.

It wasn't not cute.

I leaned onto his lap and laid my head down. From here, I could see the rat.

"I like you, but your timeline is sucking a lot of ass right now.

"That's because you're the smartest fucking one in it."

"Aw, you say the nicest cop stuff."

"Isn't your future all messed up because of that Mitchel kid?

"No, we got past that. It was about a hundred years of chaos and bullshit, but we built it back up. A lot of people died who didn't have to, though. And if you can avoid going through shit like that, definitely do it. I recommend it."

"So, your time is ok? What's the Nuclear Demon thing?

"I don't know. Strawberry said it. It could be a different timeline than mine."

"Did the vest look similar?"

"Yeah, just a little older. He said it was his dad's."

"So, this guy was from..."

"2612."

"And you're from..."

"2540."

"Ok, he's seventy-two years after you, trying to stop a Nuclear Demon. And his face was all red, kind of like a sunburn or other kind of burn."

"Oh, shit. This isn't relaxing anymore." I sat up.

"The Nuclear Demon thing happens after my time. Fuck."

"So, what do you do about that?"

"I don't know. This is an unusual case. I go back in time to make timelines that will trend and carry positive resolutions across to other branching timelines. I don't deal with shit that happens in the future. That's for people after me."

"So, none of it's familiar?"

"No."

Davi poked her head in the front cab, "Hey, guys, the people in this house say we need to take this thing out of here if we want it."

She handed Albio the keys.

Los was really enjoying bouncing up and down in the kitchen area as the RV made its way to a less populated area. Every once in a while, a big bump would thrust his head up into the bottom of the microwave and he'd laugh.

Sean was waiting his turn.

Davi put her head down and was pretending to sleep. None of us could sit still. It looked like the one major defect of RV living was that no one could really accomplish anything while the fucking thing was moving.

I checked on Albio.

"So, how's it going? You know? With the road."

"As soon as I get this thing up to 20, it starts shaking really, really hard."

He wasn't wrong. That thing was shaking like a gap toothed stripper at a high priced dental convention. For more cutesy sayings like that, check out my OnlyFans site.

As I walked back, the three of them were sitting in a row.

Davi bounced a little. "We need to talk."

"Is this an intervention?"

Sean shot back, "Probably. In a way. No."

"Ok, I'm glad we cleared that up."

Davi continued, "the elephant in the room is that we saw a different you back at the bar. Another you."

"I think that was an illusion."

Los tried to stand up. "We have theories."

"Oh, fuck me. This should be interesting." I sat down. "Let's hear 'em."

They looked at each other.

Los was excited, "Idea one. We were all concentrating so hard on you and stuff that we all fantasized and then just saw you in your undies. It was hot. That's all."

He sat back down.

"Ok, Murder She Wrote. If that's true, how cum I just threw up?"

Los stood back up,

"Because that can be sexy sometimes, too."

"Buzz. Sorry. You lose your turn. Forever. How about you, Nancy Drew?"

"How do you know all these old timey references?"

"Jesus. Mod squad, what part of Time Traveler do you not understand?" I've BEEN to the past. I admit that, as a black woman, it all sucked, but I did my time, Octavia Butler style. Now you, go, DAVINA."

"Ok, that was a different version of you coming back to that point to check on why the vest didn't work. You were looking from behind. It's a different angle. It was research."

"Ok, Olivia Benson, but I wasn't wearing a vest, was I? My titties were out. I'm not currently wearing underwear, and, again, sick."

Davi looked up and considered.

"Ok, now you, Point Break. Straight talk. What do you think happened?"

"Ah. I think that the vest malfunctioned and pulled a version of you into that time instead of pushing you into a different time. And it found a version that was alone and open, but the whole thing made you sick."

"Ok, this is not bad. So what you're saying is that the vest works, it's just working wrong?"

"Yes."

I looked at Davi. "I'm sorry, babe. You know you're my bitch, but I think Lego Thor over here may be closest."

Sean nodded at the group, "I have a big head."

Davi looked at me. "Have you ever seen a malfunction like that?"

"No. But I'm going to take it apart and find out."

I realized the bouncing had stopped.

Albio walked back.

"You guys should see something."

We piled out of the RV. I had forgotten that real atmosphere existed. I made a note to air that fucking thing out.

"We're in a forest. We barely drove at all?" I looked at Albio.

He shrugged. "This is why people live in Peoria. You're always like five minutes away from a forest."

"Weird."

"But that's not what you should look at." He handed me a pair of binoculars and pointed me.

Looking through the binoculars, I could see across the forest to a small clearing about a mile away. There were tents around a central bonfire. I adjusted them so they were a little more clear. A man dressed in blue stood near the fire counting. As I panned, I could see what he was counting. There were about twenty boys, all dressed in boy scout uniforms.

And off to one side, was fucking Mitchel Wagner.

Top five ways I know that the universe wants me to kill Mitchel Wagner

1. Proximity

I was dropped into a swimming pool about six blocks away from his house when I first got to this timeline. Impressive aim, really, but does it mean anything? I mean, I'm near people all the time that I don't kill. I have such insane self-control I've lived next door to people and still haven't killed them. They were even DJs. Proximity alone means nothing.

2. Redirection

The one time I was specifically driving AWAY from Mitchel Wagner's home, the universe dropped a fucking cow on the van. That shit didn't even happen in the bible. God didn't stop Saul by chucking farm animals at him. Comparatively, he was very chill. And Saul changed his FUCKING NAME because of that shit. I turned around, but I'm not changing my name to Paula.

3. Busted Shit

When I tried to jet the fuck out of here without killing Mitchel Wagner, the vest stopped working and won't start again. Is it broken until I kill this fucker? Or is there a different reason? Can I not leave until I stick a knife up this kid's cunt? Jesus.

4. Proximity (part 2)

We drove out to the fucking forest and there he was with his whole boy scout troupe, just waiting to get his ass killed. Of all the forests we could have driven to, that's the one we ended up in. Seriously, Peoria is surrounded by four-thousand calming forest glens, the overwhelming majority of which do not contain psychopathic boy scouts. But here we fucking are.

5. Identity

The universe made him a goddamn boy scout, the single most killable kind of thing on the planet. If you see a boy scout and don't want to punch its fucking lights out, you are a strange breed of people, Tito, because the little blues make me see red. That is all. Fuck.

"Do you believe that?"

"Ah. Fuck. I said that out loud again, didn't I?"

Davi nodded. "The universe really wants you to kill a fourteen-year-old boy?"

"I guess so. To be clear, the universe itself kills fourteen-year-old boys all the time. I would be more of an in-between."

"A facilitator," Sean offered.

"Exactly."

"Please don't, sweetheart." She shushed him.

Albio stood next to Davi, "There has to be another way. Really."

I looked up. Where was Los?

Sean called out, "Dude."

"Oh, here."

We jumped up as he stepped from behind me holding some papers, ruffling through them.

"What the fuck, tiny Santana?"

"Your little Mitchel whelp is there, for sure, see," he pointed to his name on the sheet. We could talk about the word "whelp" later.

"Did you run down there and steal the attendance sheets?"

"And menu requirements. Mitchel is lactose intolerant. I think lactose intolerance is still intolerance."

He held his fist up, like Fred Hampton. So did Sean. I leaned over and put the fists down and grabbed the papers.

"It is him for sure?" Davi looked worried.

I looked through the papers. "Hold on. There's three. Mitchel Wagner, Robert McCade, Donald Robeson. Of the five, there are three."

Albion looked over, "Are you sure?"

"I'm absolutely sure. I can never forget those names. Mitchel Wagner, Junior Senator from Illinois, Robert McCade, Illinois Circuit Judge, Donald Robeson, Assistant District Attorney. Three out of five"

"And that's their titles when it happens?"

"Yep. And then Wagner becomes President, it gets out, War."

Davi looked resolute, "The three of them may be here for a reason. Maybe the job should be to move them in a different direction. So they don't do it?"

"So, we need to go down there and teach three teenage boys about consent?"

"Is it that crazy?"

"Honestly. No, it's not. I'm not super crazy about shooting up a jamboree, myself. But, fuck. How do you stop them from growing up and getting their tiny little rape merit badges?"

"We go down there, kill everyone ELSE, take the three boys, and then, over the next thirty years or so, raise them ourselves to be kind, compassionate, and maybe gay." Los was waving his hands, painting the whole thing for us.

I sat down in the dirt.

"Well, that's a plan, too..."

Albio kneeled right next to me.

"I had something else to show you, too, actually."

Albio led me from behind while I closed my eyes. Why do I trust people?

"If you walk me off a cliff, I'll kick your ass."

"Ok, open your eyes."

I did. In front of us was a wide pond surrounded by bushes and trees. But while most other ponds in the forest might have been brown and gray with sediment, this one looked blue and pristine. It didn't seem natural.

"What is this?"

"I don't know. I found it last year. I camp up here a lot, by myself. I think they were trying to dig a pool for people to use and stopped halfway through. The ground is compact and sealed, and it's pretty even across the whole thing. But it's still natural. I mean, it's not a sink in a gender neutral bar bathroom, but…"

"I dig it. You don't want to bring the other guys?"

"How about we do that tomorrow? I thought that maybe tonight we could hang out?"

He put his hands on the small of my back and kissed me.

"Yeah? No sinks, huh?"

"Can you do without?"

"I can try." I leaned into the kiss that time.

And the next.

You don't really need the details at that time. I think you've probably heard enough about my fucking sex life by now. I will tell you I got water in all my places, but I'm sure you can figure that out.

We fell asleep wrapped up together.

It was almost worth the whole trip.

I woke up to Davi shaking me. I shot up and nearly stepped on Albio's dick.

"I'm here. Here." He stood up slowly, protecting the parts.

She looked frantic.

"You gotta come here."

We made our way quickly back to the RV. I was looking for the two action figures we travel with, but they were gone. Davi shook her head.

"This way."

We moved around to the front of the RV and there they were, looking like cats who ate the dog. Right behind them was a girl with a shaved head and a savage expression on her face. She was tied up naked.

I took a breath. "This isn't a BDSM thing?"

Sean looked pleased with himself. "The same tie you used for him."

He pointed at Albio. I felt my heart drop

He leaned in and whispered to me.

"You see the problem with this whole thing now, right?"

I put my hand on his face and pushed. "Can you take Beavis and Beaviser away from here for a few?"

Albio grabbed the guys and left me and Davi alone with her. I leaned over.

"This is going to take some splaining. If I take off the tape, will you let me do that?" I tried to sound comforting.

She nodded quickly. I pulled the tape off and started. As I did, Davi pointed to the pile of clothing. On top of it was a time vest. It was a different color and a bit newer than mine, but it was absolutely a time vest.

I took a deep breath.

"Ok, I'm from 2540. I'm on the Mitchel Wagner thing and I'm trying to figure out how to proceed. My vest doesn't work right now and I connected with these fine people here to try and follow through on all this. I'm sort of in a regroup phase right now, so depending on why you are here, maybe we can share some intel. These guys panicked when they saw you and clearly went dick up about all of it. I apologize, and I'm sure we can work out how to move forward."

For what it's worth, talking like that for too long really hurts my head. Fuck this. If gender swapped Jason Statham over here wants to fuck my life up because Shaggy and Scrappy saw her hoo haw, I'm really just too tired to manifest a gassy fuck about it. I wanted to say that. But I'm a paragon of fucking restraint. So, ok, bitch. Now you talk.

And a stream of words came out of her mouth that were in some language I've never heard before. The only words I recognized were "Mitchel" and 'Wagner". I stood up.

Davi folded her arms, "Did you get any of that?"

I sighed.

"Not a fucking word."

Chapter Six:

The Universe has no HR Department

"Can I not be naked right now?"

She sat on the ground in front of us in a blanket with her time vest draped over her shoulder. In the last fifteen minutes, Davi and I had found some things out.

5 things quickly.

1. The universe has no HR department. Sucks to be her. Stripping and tying her up was the most work any hippies have done in the last forty years. There was no one to Karen to about it.

2. Her time vest includes a translator. Cool deal. That would have saved me some time in the first century on my first mission as I tried to play charades in Aramaic. I almost got my hands cut off by some giant Moroccan guy who said he was Jesus' brother-in-law and he owed him money. The bible leaves a lot out.

3. She comes from a time a bit later than me, but a divergent timeline where the Dutch actually won a war. So, real fucking divergent.

4. She is speaking Dutch. Which is not, as far as I can tell, the language of love.

5. She prefers wearing clothing.

"There is really no way to sit when you're naked without the little roll things happening and I work out."

"Clearly." She actually was pretty impressive. But body insecurity? Come on.

"Ok, what's your name?"

"My name is Blu Aafjes." She nodded at the panties. I handed them to her. She shimmied into them with her hands still tied. Blu Aafjes sounded like the airplane service ABBA used in their 1980 Tour of Nova Scotia.

"And you are..."

"I'm a subtractionist." I nodded and she pointed her foot at the skirt. I helped her put it on. She lifted her butt.

"This is for the rest of the whole pile of clothes. Listen closely for all of it. Here goes. Are you here to kill a boy scout?"

She looked up at me and Davi. This one could be a yes or no question. She tried to get a feel for our take on this situation. The problem is this was no longer "pro-sociopathic rapist" or "anti-sociopathic rapist." There were apparently gray areas.

"Aren't you?"

That pretty much told me what I needed to know.

"I'm going to give you all the clothes and untie you. You, in turn, have to promise not to kill anyone till we figure this out, and not to maim our idiots. Capisce?"

She nodded. I tried to remember if that meant the same in Dutch.

The guys came back from the other side of the RV. She looked at Sean and Los and flipped them off.

"Fuck you, losers."

Sean looked impressed. "You taught her English. That was so fast."

Los nodded, "She sounds like you now."

Albio joined in, "I call for an updated policy against stripping and tying up people."

As much as I hated this situation, I liked the policy the way it was.

"Nope," I stepped over to Albio. "So, what is going on with the boys from Brazil?"

"Well, your sociopathic dictator monster is trying to earn his cooking merit badge by scrambling some artificial eggs over the little fire that could."

"Her vest doesn't work, either." I pointed at the girl from Star Trek: The Motion Picture and sighed.

"And it stopped two days ago?"

"She thinks."

Albio paused for a second. He looked pained. "Can I ask a shitty question?"

"You can ask…"

"Is it possible that you were floating in that pool for longer than you think?"

"You think I got here two days ago, not one."

I turned to Davi, "What made you guys notice that I was in the pool when I first got here?

She looked up, to think. I felt like this would be bad.

Los jumped in. "That was me. I went to wash my hands in the pool because Sean was in the bathroom, and the kitchen sink didn't work because we're trying to raise fish."

I turned back to Albio.

"Could have been two days."

"Wait, so you guys aren't going to kill Wagner?" Blue was pulling on her boots. She was wearing her vest as a backpack now, making her look even more like if Tank Girl had fucked Dora the Explorer and had a lanky bald ass baby.

Davi spoke up, "Serendipity Express."

"Yup." This was the issue right now. The Universe wants it too bad. Suspicious.

"Fuck," Furiosa kicked a rock surprisingly far. She walked past me and pushed Los, knocking him over, and then proceeded to sit down against the left front wheel well of the RV, facing away from us.

Albio shrugged. "I didn't like you guys either, when I first... you know."

"Honestly, we don't make a good first impression."

I walked over to her and kicked her foot.

"Hey, Bubblicious. Wanna help me do some tests?"

So, when I say that the Universe has "software," people don't really pay attention to everything that goes into that shit. One of the things that software does is it sort of "stamps" things with information that identifies something about that thing's origins. In nature, there are literally hundreds of these "stamps" that can be read later if you know how to look for them.

The one you're probably familiar with is carbon dating. This is when you start with an idea of the normative carbon levels for something and then take a look at the carbon isotopes in the thing to see how much that varies. The job is, like, "This is how much fucking carbon should be in a living duck dinosaur, breathing carbon."

Now, kill that big ass bird and it's not taking in carbon anymore. Wait a million years and test again. So, you figure out the half-lives of these various isotopes and determine when that mummy died, or if that creature is really an ancient alien, or if that shroud choked Jesus to death. It essentially pulls out a time map and says "You belong here, motherfucker. Big red X."

Background radiation, genetic profiles, quantum laws and behaviors, etc. all of these things diverge in different timelines. You can build a machine called a Variegator™ that averages all of these things out and decides what timeline you belong on. Absent a map of those timelines, you can at least use it to determine if two things belong to the same timeline. A Variegator™ will also measure the standing energy of a timeline, so you can do a couple of tests for one low low price. It's got some heft, so you can also clock someone over the head with it, which may be a usage that comes up later. Right now, I'm primarily concerned with the first two uses.

Since we're talking like this, I feel like this may be a good time for me to insert this here:

The History of Time Travel in Five Glorious Parts:

1. Time Travel is Theorized.

So, this guy, Professor Ronald Mallet, works at the University of Connecticut. He theorizes, as we said earlier, that using a spiral laser to swirl up some spacetime can help you travel in time. The idea is that spacetime is connected and is affected by light and gravity. Imagine you stir a cup of coffee vigorously with your masturbatin' hand. Certain particles of coffee that might never have touched each other may now come into contact. Ron Mallett found that the spoon can be tiny and made out of light. Oh, and that spacetime is like coffee, I guess.

2. Time travel is invented. Sort of.

So, Ron Mallett tries to get time travel that can benefit mankind in so many ways funded. No one will give him money. He even starts a GoFundMe page, which almost makes as much money as the one that girl from Parks and Rec started for her boob job. Still, it's not enough. I mean, it was enough for the boob job. That happened and it looked great. But not enough for time travel. So, about two-hundred years go by. A company called REPLAY is started by an idiot billionaire who wants to suck his own dick. He funds this technology and starts sending people back in time one day to fuck themselves. I'm not being unkind. "Come Fuck Yourself" was basically their tagline. The people who guided you into the very recent past so you could stick your dick in infinity were called "Replay Arts Trainers" or "Rats." This whole era was, by the way, suspiciously uneventful as billionaires decided, en masse, that rather than die in low earth orbit spaceship explosions and tiny undersea tube submarine implosions, they would waste that time, money, and energy in temporal auto-fellation.

3. Time travel hits a snag.

Millions of dollars later, some odd behaviors started popping up. People fucking themselves not being odd enough, I guess. For many of the short, uneventful engagements, everything worked fine. But if people stayed too long and their timeline diverged too much from their original timeline, they ended up returning to the future of that timeline and not the original. This meant people would disappear, but in the target timeline, there would be a slightly older and a slightly younger version of themselves. And, again, the universe DIDN'T CARE. If there were six-million versions of Ted in six million timelines and they all ended up cohabitating in a single timeline with their dicks up their assholes in a mass Daisy Chain of Freedom®, the universe is cool with that.

It turns out, though, that losing billionaires is a bad business model. So REPLAY ended up pivoting.

4. Time travel as SAS.

They sold the technology to the UN as a service. Surprising absolutely no one, the UN decided that it could do better things with it. They opened a Retcon Agency and hired some people to go back in time and make terrible things not happen. They called these people "subtractionists" because their jobs were to remove evil shit. And they went to work. It turned out, though, that time travel didn't really change the existing timeline. Or at last the way they thought it would. The bad stuff they tried to stop still happened. But as they sent more and more people after it, they found that the bad stuff seemed, well... less bad. So, for example, they sent people to eliminate Hitler. A bunch of them succeeded, but that just changed things moving forward on THAT timeline, not the one they were sent from. And if it became too divergent, that agent would be lost, returning to the timeline they impacted. But as more and more timelines didn't have Nazis, some people started remembering things a little differently. And some books were a little different. And the problem of Neonazi fascists in the present seemed to diminish. What they had done was to decrease the percentage of timelines with Nazis in ratio to the ones without. And those timelines began to run together more closely, sometimes creating confluences.

5. Time Travel as Reality.

So, the agents, who now called themselves "Retcon Agency Tools" or "Rats" as a joke, started to approach this not as a "one and done" kind of adventure, but as a more subtle enterprise.

We weren't "eliminating Nazism," we were "chipping away at it". It was like the past was a sculpture and we were reshaping it, across the entire span of timelines. What we did was still important. And sometimes you got to see a ton of people not get unalived, which was honestly worth it. If you made a timeline substantially better, too, you got to live in it. Which is why we joke about rats leaving sinking ships. Which also happens a la the Titanic and that Ratatouille movie.

I held up the Variegator™ for everyone to see outside the side door of the RV in my most Lion King-esque pose. Davi, Los, and Sean were sunbathing, and Albio was leaning against a tree waiting. They had, apparently, all made really good use of their time while I was working.

"It looks like Caillou and I are from the same timeline."

Sean and Los applauded. Davi sat up, "That doesn't make sense. Do people speak Dutch where you come from?"

I handed the Variegator™ over to my lab partner and continued.

"No. And no self-respecting human being speaks Dutch. But I also found that this is a massively High Energy timeline. We are in the biggest confluence I've ever seen. So, it looks like our timelines may have just trended and joined like tributaries meeting back up. Does that sound about right, dodgeball?"

Suddenly, the light glinted off her head as she bolted toward the slight hill that led to the boy scout encampment. She passed Albio and slammed the Variegator™ as hard as possible into his ear. He folded like a pinochle table and she took off running faster than I'd ever seen a human go - even the people with no legs who have those bouncy metal things.

I admit it was impressive.

I took off after her, but it was probably hopeless. I saw Davi and the guys follow, but I was ahead of them.

I hoped Albio was okay, but as I ran the numbers in my brain, I realized that we were now both at two bouts of unconsciousness in as many days. I really should have been concerned about my own neurological health. Put your own mask on first, they say.

It was about a mile to run, so we both started to lose gas about two-hundred feet away from camp. I caught up to her and just breathed heavily for a little bit. Finally, I said, "I got you now."

"Shhh."

She was staring at the encampment. We started walking closer. There were big puffs of black smoke rising up. As we approached, we could see in the clearing boy scouts lying on the ground, many decapitated, all dead. Scoutmasters had been ripped apart, the entire field was muddy with blood.

And trudging through it were eight or nine shapes wearing time vests. They moved with slow and delicate precision across the field putting holes in bodies that were already dead. They were about six foot tall and nearly the same width across sitting atop single spherical wheels that looked to be magnetically attached.

Robots.

Blu and I walked back to camp and talked. Her translator attached an extra millisecond or two of time to every back and forth, interrupting the flow a bit, but not so much as to overturn the conversation.

She opened, "So, you don't have robot subtractionists, either?"

"We don't even have Dutch as a language anymore."

"Ouch. When do you think they were from?"

"I don't know, really."

I didn't.

She walked past Albio when we were near the RV. She turned to me, ignoring him completely.

"I'm sorry I knocked out your boyfriend."

He looked up, wiping blood from his ear.

"Thank you, bitch."

I shrugged at him. "I don't know that we've really, you know, defined the relationship." He was shaking his head, trying to clear all the excess blood. What was it about this guy that hit me like a can of Orange Monster and a gas station boner pill? He was like a human ruffie.

I looked around. I really hope I hadn't said that out loud.

"I get it. I broke up with my girlfriend to take this mission."

"She had hair?"

"No. I mean, yes, but... I just knew I'd never see her again."

Los came up behind us and patted her on the head,

"You know, AI is probably going to take my job away, too. I'm sorry."

He rubbed her head a bit and then went to find more vitamins.

"I'm going to kill that one. That's a freebie."

Davi was naked. She'd been tanning. This was apparently commonplace because I didn't see any tanlines on her smooth light brown freckled skin. I suddenly felt super gay. She cleared her throat.

"Yes, sorry."

"So, you didn't kill those boy scouts?"

"No, they were pre-killed."

Albio handed me the binoculars.

"Check this out."

The robots were all just standing there. They hadn't returned home or moved on or anything. They just... stood there.

I looked at Blu and passed the binoculars back to the ruffie.

"Do you think they can't get back, either?"

"Maybe no vest works right now. For anyone."

"Or...." Albio was still looking.

"What? What is happening?"

He passed the binoculars. "I have no idea."

As I kept looking, it became clear they were doing something. At first, I thought they were burrowing into the ground.

"Are they melting?"

Blu grabbed the binoculars from me. These things were getting around.

"Right. Why bother bringing robots home? Do the job, self-destruct."

"Or... they CAN'T bring them back home anymore?"

"Maybe the thing with the vests is localized to here? They can send people here, but no one can leave?"

Davi whistled. "Hey, guys. We're going to the pool to swim and get fucked up. We're done for the day. Are you guys coming?"

I looked at Albio. He shrugged. I'd been in the camper of doom most of the day with shinyhappyhead analyzing things and inhaling piss fumes, so I felt done.

He looked at me

"You want to go get high?"

So, first we got high as fuck.

Los passed a joint around in a circle and we all eased into the ground. It was a beautiful night. I looked over at Davi and she was cuddled up against Sean and if I squinted I could see what she saw in him. He was fun. He was affirmative. He just said "yes" to shit.

We swam for a while, splashing around and laughing. Blu tried to drown Los, but I think that got less purposeful as the day went on. I gave Albio a handie in the water like a seventh grader, and we made out for a bit. I think I might have made out with Davi, too, if i'm being totally honest. She tasted like sugary cinnamon cereal.

I floated for a while, trying to figure out what to do next.

Back in my own time, I worked for the UN, so I could live anywhere. I had nothing to tie me down, so I chose my hometown of Norico, Portugal and just let myself sort of sink into it. No partner, no friends, just missions. This was the closest thing I ever had to time off.

I need to get home, but maybe not right away.

Not now. I was flopped on the ground right by the water. To my left, Albio was on top of Blu having sex. I tapped her on the shoulder, and she turned her head to me. I could see her lips just a few inches away from mine.

"You Know, me and cheekbones here are total whores. But are you usually this big of a whoremonster?"

She looked thoughtful for a moment while rocking back and forth, belly full of dick.

"No. I don't think so."

"Hm." I looked at my hand. It was beautiful. That was one good looking hand. Davi rolled over and put her mouth on my belly. She licked my belly button. It felt really good. She put her hands on my ass and started moving down

"Lower. Lower." I pushed her head down and we laughed. She put her mouth on me and it felt so warm and wet. She started licking.

I looked up and saw Sean standing there with Los between his legs, sucking on his dick. He opened his mouth really wide and a stream of rainbows came out. His voice was booming and the ground shook.

"You are the light of the world, Kerys. And his message is light." He spread his hands out as though he was getting ready to take off. I was never that used to hearing my own name. When I was young, the one phrase that could always shut me down immediately was "Focus, Kerys." And the hard part of that is that one of those words was my actual own name.

I focused.

Suddenly, Sean's head opened up. I could see light pouring out from inside it. There was a kind of rhythm to the light. In my mind I felt like I could understand it. Like a morse code. It felt like the entrance for a vocalist on tour.

I saw fingers first, then the top of a tiny green head. As it lifted itself up, a small green alien popped out in a little spaceship, from his head. It was more Kazoo than Giger. It seemed to have a layer of light down all over it, soft, cuddly. The alien stood up on the ship. It pulled out a glowing map and pointed to it. The movements were in the same rhythm as the pulsing lights.

I mouthed silently, "Who uses paper maps anymore...?"

It shrugged and started rapping.

"Like a tiny garden gnome." The alien was breathing heavily. Its eyes narrowed. "Gnome" echoed.

The beat built along with the lightshow.

It whispered.

"I just got to get home…" The final word reverberated and pulsed. The alien crossed its arms, and I saw a tiny mic fall to the floor and bounce once before laying still.

Then I came really hard.

I opened my eyes. It was dark.

I was wrapped around Davi, still naked. I extricated myself without waking her up. Blu and Albio were splashing in the water. I jumped in and tackled him and he laughed.

Blu splashed the both of us. "What the fuck was in that?"

I leaned in to Albio and splashed her back, "Oh, you liked it, whore."

I grabbed Albio's head. "And how's your head, little manwhore?"

"Surprisingly good."

Los slid into the water. "It's called fourstar. It's my homage to Chicago.

I splashed him, too. "So, what did you poison us with, bitch?"

He held up four fingers and counted down.

The Ingredients to Los' famous FourStar weed cocktail

1. Marijuana

The most beautiful and well-crafted Strain of Northern Lights Jimmy Jam Marijuana.

2. Orange Kool-Aid

Adds a bit of sweetness and bite to the mix. Do not forget.

3. Ecstasy

Don't think we need to go into too much detail here.

4. Ketamine

Because why not, people.

Blu stared at me. "Jesus, man."

Sean had scuttled over to Davi and was cuddling next to her.

The four of us climbed back onto the bank and sat in a circle while Los rolled another joint.

I looked at the three of them and I tried to imagine them moving closer.

Suddenly, my tunnel vision cleared. I could see perfectly.

I grabbed the joint and inhaled.

Los inhaled and held his breath. He leaned over and put his face down on Albio's cock. It seemed to happen entirely in slow motion. I touched Albio and Blu's feet with my own and felt a connection, like a circuit.

Albio took a hit and blew it into Blu's mouth. She inhaled and started kissing him. He played with her tits while she took a hit.

"Just so you guys know, I was born a male." She leaned over and blew smoke in my mouth. I took the joint and held it, kissing her.

Albio laughed. "I was born a baby. But shit changes."

At that moment, this was the funniest thing any of us had ever heard. I held the joint in my hand. Davi had slid her panties on me, but I could still feel the wet grass under me. It felt amazing.

I watched Albio arch his back a little and I wondered how long until he came. He and Blu were kissing and she was motioning me to come over.

But in that moment, I couldn't move. It was darker now, but lights still swirled around my head, brightly colored and beautiful. I could feel my skin stretched taut all over my body and it was pulsing with the little bits of water clinging to it. I felt like all my atoms were talking to me all at the same time, and if I listened together, without trying to separate them in my head, it was like a harmony. I tried to make my body move, but it wouldn't, and that was ok. I didn't want to push it.

It felt like it was where it needed to be.

Los sat up and took the joint from me. He was laughing.

Blu climbed on top of Albio and I suddenly felt connected to her through him. Her lower back seemed to move and dip like water as she slid up and down on his cock. And every time she slid down, there was a bright flash of light and what felt like a tiny boom in the air, like a basketball bounced in a giant room.

Los took a hit and started laughing. He leaned in and blew smoke into Blu's mouth, then into Albio's. The smoke seemed to pick up the light from the impacts and coil, stopping in space for a second, then billowing with every boom.

I tried to close my eyes and feel it, but they wouldn't close. Albio's hands curled around her back and I could feel him cumming through the air between us. The boom that accompanied his orgasm extended and didn't fade. It was like it was looped until it became a tiny whir. The light shook and wrapped around me until I couldn't see through it.

And then suddenly, I could.

I was in the Owl's Nest bar staring at myself in a time vest. I looked so beautiful, and so did Davi and the rest in the bar. I saw Albio's eyes dart from the other me to me, and I could suddenly feel what he felt.

It felt like love.

My mouth finally opened.

"Very nice."

And I threw up all over myself.

Chapter Seven:

Prometheus Explained

"Dude, liking this Breaking Bad™ thing."

Los was excited to be using the RV for what he considered to be its rightful function. But not everyone was. Pan that way.

To the left.

Over there.

Yep.

Davi's arms were folded. "You can't possibly think that you time traveled because you got a little high."

Sean laughed, "I've done it mult- "

Davi put her hand in Sean's mouth as far as it would go. Surprisingly far. Like almost up to the wrist. I thought for a minute that Sean might be bigger on the inside than the outside, like a tesseract or a tardis or something. I'll lab that one up later.

"I'm not making any judgments right now. I'm trying to figure this shit out without shaking my head too much or changing my Y axis at all because I feel like him."

I pointed to Albio who had wrapped a hoodie entirely around his head and was sprawled on the couch like a sunburned starfish. "I'm good."

Sinead poked her head in. She was glistening and had wrapped her vest around her neck like one of those golf course fratboy rape polos. "You guys good?"

"Oh, sweet fuck... are you jogging?" This fucking monster was jogging.

"Just trying to clear my head from the... are you guys ok?"

The guys mouthed and nodded "yes."

"No. I woke up without the use of my hands. I think I permanently forgot my middle name. How the fuck are you jogging?"

Los nodded approvingly, "We're cooking up a new batch."

Blu stepped up into the RV like a pencil eraser being shoved up an asshole, "Can I watch?"

I did a Queen Elizabeth over the table for her, "This is what we are dealing with." On the table was the various contents of FourStar.

Los bounced his head back and forth, "Well, not everything?"

"This is everything you said."

"Orange Kool-Aid."

I pointed to the Kool-Aid packets sitting there and grunted.

Los laughed, "Oh, you... oh. You thought I meant just orange Kool-Aid."

I tilted my head to look at him. My right frontal lobe detached and slid to the left side, pinching the Broca's area a little, preventing me from speaking.

"No one just drinks Kool-Aid. On its own, it's a shitty drink."

"Mmmbee," Sean said.

I pulled Davi's wet hand out of Sean's mouth.

"LSD. You don't make Kool-Aid without LSD."

Blu was looking at her hands. "I had LSD."

"Yes, little Dutch girl, but you were already fucking crazy." She kept staring at her hands. I wondered what she was seeing. I looked at her and mouthed, "Stop that."

Albio was not moving. I gave his foot a little kick.

"Hi, everyone. Just keeping my head from falling off."

Davi looked around. "So, to be clear, did anyone else here besides Kerys 'go' anywhere last night?"

"Why didn't I travel, too? I mean, I'm a traveler." Blu asked.

Everyone was skeptical.

"Ok, I want you guys to remember something. When I bought these jeans and shirt, I didn't get any underwear. I wasn't wearing any when we saw future me at the Owl's Nest in a pair of what? Black panties. But future me was wearing a pair of black panties."

"Which were mine." Davi added.

"Which were hers. None of us could have known that."

Sean raised his hand, "I figured you two would be doing it at some point."

"Except Sean, who had it all worked out in his little PornHubby brain."

"So, we're going to get high and try again?" Davi asked.

"I'm out of options, kitty cat," I sighed.

Blu pulled out a flyer from her vest pocket and slid it over. "This was at the book store on the way back."

I looked at her as though she had grown four entirely new arms. "You stopped at the book store, too? Didn't you? You read something. You jogged and then you read something."

"Seriously, this may be option A?"

I looked down.

Wednesday, 7PM - 9

Join us for a discussion of the possibilities of time travel with world famous author and Physicist Dr. Ronald Mallett from the University of Connecticut.

University of Chicago Bookstore and Cafe

I looked at Davi who was nodding like one of those spring loaded big headed baseball player novelty figures.

"A hundred-and-seventy miles away."

I rubbed Albio's head while he sat in the driver's seat. He was feeling better.

He looked down. "We're in an RV that has a quarter-of-a-million miles on it."

"Aww. They went to the moon."

"What a nice family trip," he countered.

"Well, moonie, I think we're about to add a hundred-and-seventy more."

"Are we good driving AWAY from Mitchel Wagner? Is there a risk of cow?"

"My guess is that now he and his little buddies are dead, we're all good. Wow. I just got real comfortable with the deaths of a bunch of fourteen-year-olds."

"Well. He's supposed to be a monster, so…"

"Still. Hm."

"How's your vibration tolerance?"

"Good, Ima find something to rub on." I was definitely crashing.

"You know," he dropped his voice. "I'm okay with boyfriend as a title. I know it's been just a couple of days, but…"

"Oh, honey. Honeybear. Poo Poo Bear." I sat in his lap. "My people… are so much more advanced than yours. At most you could be a cherished and beloved pet."

"So, you'd pet me and feed me and stuff?"

I kissed his cheeks. "Oh, I'd take care of you. I'm not a monster." I put my mouth on his and just let it rest there as our lips opened together. I let my tongue fall into his mouth and it felt good. His hands wrapped around me and slid between my legs and I rubbed myself against him. "Groom you. Express your anal glands."

"But no bark," I slapped him across the face and he smiled. I could hear his heartbeat double.

Dutch Asian Jada came up front just as I had squirted myself into the passenger seat like jack-off lotion out of an old bottle.

"He's my pet now," I said seriously.

There was a short delay while her translator worked it out, "Well, he fucks like an animal, so."

I reached up to feel her face. It was there. "I told him that our people were so much more advanced, baby doll."

"So, young lady, did our people get any sleep at all?"

"I don't operate on sleep. I run on sunlight and drugs, babycakes."

Yeah, I don't know where that came from. Also, why do I call people some version of "baby" when I'm tired? We never really can dig deeply enough into our own traumas.

She picked me up from the seat. "Yeah, I'm going to find a human bed for your owner."

Albio turned, "Woof woof." He started driving.

And everything sort of faded out.

Home

A few years before I was born, people all over the Earth started celebrating the year 2500. It was a nice big round number, so people were just chewing it up. The celebration dragged on for years, actually, and a lot of people stayed drunk the whole time. It was sort of the dark ages for the service industry because, for real, no one gave a fuck about showing up to do anything.

People spoke in hushed tones about having to make their own tacos.

"Let's do it up, big," said literally everyone at the same time, mostly slurring their words.

So they did.

There was this Portugese band that played wild dance music in Spanish.

I know. Why not Portuguese?

Well, about two-hundred years earlier the leaders of Spain and Portugal had a bet. And I am not making this shit up. The bet was over when a storm would hit. Someone might have been drunk. Definitely someone had a gambling problem. Anyway, Portugal lost and had to make Spanish their national language.

This pissed off a lot of people for decades, and then, one day, everyone stopped caring.

Remember this sentence, because you will see it again if you are a student of human nature.

At any rate, this band was called Gemelocos, which was a combination of the word "gemelos" or "twins" and "locos" or "crazy." There were three members of this band, the Crazy Twins.

Just let it roll off you. It can't hurt you.

They used a funding website called "GIMME" to raise money for a first tier world class music festival on the night right before the new century. People who donated would get tickets.

The first week, they raised a shitload of money. The plan was to have the festival in a place called Porto Covo, Portugal.

I probably don't need to translate that for you. It's a port and a cove.

So, the population of Porto Covo was about five-thousand people. This was up from the 1,200 or so in the 21st century. Some fastidious breeding, I suspect. The Gemelocos decided to gift the residents of Porto Covo with a percentage of ticket sales for this conference.

Half the ticket money would go to them.

So, this mysterious hacker group called "The Boot of Destiny" got involved. They wanted to make the residents rich. So, they wrote a computer virus. For the next six months, everybody in the world who wanted to buy ANYTHING online had to unclick a box, or else they would automatically donate to the Gimme page.

These donations were relative to the purchase. So, buy a house online, donate big.

Unless you unchecked the box.

It probably won't surprise you that about eighty percent of purchasers were too lazy to uncheck a box.

Soon, this Gimme fund swelled to the 21st equivalent of a billion dollars.

For a concert.

So, they want all in. Solid Gold Speakers, half a mile long zip lines leading to the stage, platinum buttplugs for the performers, name it and they bought it. It was sick. Each gift bag had a tiny endangered animal in it. Capitalismo.

But it also meant that over half the population of the planet technically had a ticket to this show. A tiny fraction of those people showed up. .001 of the population, really.

No biggie.

Twelve-million people.

And they tore that place a new asshole.

Apparently nobody was prepared for that.

Over that week, about sixty-thousand people died, five-hundred babies were born, and a couple million people got their shit fucked up. The people who lived there were not happy, despite every one of them being functional millionaires.

Gemelocos disappeared, never to be heard from again. And about a million people stayed to build a city that they called "No Rico, Pero Rico," meaning "We're not rich, but we're rich." By the time I came along, they had shortened it to Norico, and that's where I was born. I traveled, I went to college, then I chose to move back there. And my place in Norico is pretty and small and quiet, and it's a good place to come back to when some timeline fucks you up.

When you show up on the outskirts of the city, there is a sign. It has a quote on it, from, apparently, the leader of the Hacker group, "The Boot of Destiny," when he signed off forever. It just says:

"Fucking tried to do something nice, bitches."

It abbreviates to "FTTDSNB."

That is why, in my future, when someone tries to pull something off and it fucks them right in the mouth, people are known to say, "Futtitysnob."

I woke up being cuddled by Davi and Albio which, not gonna lie, didn't suck. The back bedroom no longer smelled like the inside of a used senior sized huggie, so I figured I'd gone noseblind, which was fine. I'd smelled everything I'd wanted to smell in my life. I poured one out for my entire olfactory system.

I rolled over the boy, intentionally crushing him with my ass and wandered to the front, past Sean and Los hard at work making little drugs into bigger drugs. The ping pong ball of doom was sitting behind the wheel looking through a book.

"You don't have a driver's license, woman."

"I've driven a spaceship, so..."

"Yeah, but not around Illinois state piggies while twin recidivist drug offenders were schedule oneing it in the kitchenette."

"True. I'm reading up. He's not here yet." She pointed to the bookstore across the street.

I looked at the book in her hand. A brand new copy of "How to Build a Time Machine," by Dr. Ronald Mallett. "You have money?"

"I have the will to shoplift." She smiled. "I can get it signed when he gets here."

She looked me in the eye, "Unless you want to just kidnap him, tie him up, and strip him."

"That's usually a tidy yes from me, Princess shape-of-a-peach, but I thought we could play this one a little chiller."

"Do you have a list of spherical things that you are exhausting on me? I'm half Asian. I speak Dutch. My tits could be bigger. I used to be a dude. I'm literally covered in abstract tattoos. And yet, it's the bald head you go to over and over."

I kissed her on the top of her head, "You really get me. And be nice. I'm your elder. You're twelve-years-old when I come from. Tiny little Blu."

"I feel it. Ok, I give in about an hour. How do we do this? Are we just customers?"

"I'm a fan, bitch. Aren't you?"

"Oh, yeah. But I'm not so sure that telling him we're from the future is a good idea."

Albio was rubbing his head, leaning into the front cabin of the RV from the back, "Are you guys not supposed to tell people?"

"No one believes you when you tell them," she offered up

"Yea, what she said. But it doesn't matter. The timelines are resilient as fuck. It's super hard to actually break anything."

That piqued Albio's interest. "So, if you went to a future where there was a cure for cancer and then brought it back to people, nothing would happen."

"Oh, yeah, something would happen. People in that timeline would be cancer free. The Universe doesn't give a shit about origination. Or patents. Or people for that matter."

"Right, you said that. So, it doesn't matter that no one invented it. It just exists and that's cool?"

"Yep."

"So, why don't you do that?"

Blu laughed. "For the first year, that's pretty much ALL we do."

"Yeah, just pass fire around to monkeys and shit. Why do you think every single mythology in the world has myths of godlike characters giving something cool to man?"

"Fire, the wheel, alcohol."

"Electricity, soap, wine."

"Beer, plumbing, pinatas."

"More alcohol, bananas."

"Yeah, bananas are sort of a pet project for the UN."

Albio looked confused.

She continued, "Bananas keep going extinct and not being invented and running into major dilemmas."

"They're the drama queens of the fruit and berry world."

"So, we're just constantly giving people bananas."

"It's literally a full time job," I finished.

"You've cured cancer?"

"A lot."

"Wow. you are so cool," he leaned in and kissed me. I got a kiss and all I had to do was save millions of children from bone-wrenching pain, sickness, and death. Still, not a terrible kiss.

"So the convention that you talked about? Where we meet? That's not screwing up the timelines?"

"Nope. It's grounded."

"Like, electrically?"

Davina was awake now, too. We all moved into the living area of the RV.

Snowglobe fielded this one, "Have you ever seen the movie 'Groundhog Day'?"

They all nodded. I sat next to Davi and she started massaging my neck. So, don't expect that I remembered any of this next part correctly.

"It's when that guy lives the same day over and over again."

"They make you think he's in the loop for about thirty-four years. It's probably closer to ten-thousand. But it doesn't matter. Because they have a ground."

"The ground basically puts a kink in the timeline so it loops. You can enter it and exit it, but it's continuous. And if you enter it again, you just add new versions."

"Do they do that a lot?" Davi was curious.

"Ha." This seemed to be a pet peeve of Blu's, "They cost just north of a billion dollars. So, no. it's rare."

Just then, a massive concussion almost tipped us over. I fell on the ground. We scrambled to get up and piled out of the RV toward the storefront.

People on the street were running every way. What was left of the bookstore was on fire.

I looked at Potatohead, "See? This is why no one reads anymore."

Albio and I moved in toward the front. Blu cheated around the the side while we tried to get in through the front window. The heat was intense. "Do you see anyone?"

He shook his head and wrapped his hoodie around his hands, pushing the glass in.

"Where is everyone?"

Blu came from the back holding up a tall woman who was having trouble breathing.

"She was in the alley, throwing garbage away. She says they had everyone leave so she could set up for the talk. Mallett's the only one in there."

"He's here somewhere?" I felt my fingers blister as I tried to push my way in.

"Hey," Albio called out.

I turned to him.

He pointed. "Hey. Is that your physicist?"

I squinted. About a hundred feet away, across the campus, and running right past us was Dr. Ronald Mallett.

A wave of relief washed over me.

"I wouldn't say he's mine, exactly, He belongs to the world." I looked at Albio.

"And was that...?"

"Yep." He knew right away. The guy holding his arm, dragging him away?

Well, he sort of looked like a big strawberry.

I tried to keep up with Blu this time as we followed them past Swift Hall. We caught them running around Swift Hall then running back. There was a sign that said "Swift Hall." I like to know where I'm at.

We had taken off in groups, with Albio and Davi trying to field one side, and the guys the other. As we backtracked, we lost them for just a minute, but that was all strawberry needed. Even shaped like a berry and hobbled with an uncooperative physicist, he was fast.

We heard Sean yell out. He was leaning out the door of the Starbucks trying inscrutably to whisper loudly.

"Guys. Here."

We found Los guarding the employee area like a chihuahua with a bowl of kibble.

"I think he works here." He pointed to the 'Employees only' sign.

I nodded at Los. He looked very proud of himself, so I gave him a little doggie pat.

"You can't get away," I yelled through the door, unsure if there was a way for him to get away.

"Who are you people?" I heard the Strawberry yell back.

"We're People for the Ethical Treatment of Astrophysicists, PETA. Maybe you've heard of us."

There was a pause.

"I'm not really an astrophysicist," Doctor Mallett yelled out.

"I know. I'm a huge fan. I was trying to make the letters work."

"He's fine. Now leave."

"Is everyone ok?"

Like the true leader of Academia he was, Dr. Ron was only worried about other people. I hoped it was ok to call him Dr. Ron in my head.

"No one is hurt. I mean, textbooks are gonna be a lot pricier next semester."

Albio and Davi came limping in, breathing hard.

"Campus... is so big." Albio poured himself into a chair.

Blu called out, "Just come out. We just need to talk to the professor."

"I need to talk to the professor. Go away," Strawberry whined.

"You remember us from the police station. We're not going to hurt you."

"What police station? Just go. He'll be fine."

Albio perked up. "How can he not remember us?"

"Maybe he gets tied up naked all the time."

Blu looked at me, "Ohmigod. Really?"

"We were trying to free hippies. It was a mitzvah."

Sean took a drink, "We're more free spirits than hippies."

I cocked my head, "Did you order a coffee?" I inhaled, trying to smell the pumpkin spice. Nothing. Noseblind.

There was a flash of light and a hole opened at the top of the door.

"What the fuck?"

I looked at Albio, "I didn't realize you still had that thing."

Albio shrugged.

"I have a laser gun. I'm bringing it everywhere I go."

"Ok, Jesus. We're coming out."

The door opened slowly and he came sliding out with the professor in tow.

I moved closer, "Dr. Ron, are you ok?"

"Just Ronald is good."

I looked at Strawberry, "Do you recognize that gun?"

He looked over, across all of us. "It's a laser gun. Pretty standard."

That got a look of confusion from the professor. I continued. "So that's not YOUR laser gun?"

He looked confused, "No. I left mine at home. Did you get that out of my bedroom?"

Albio raised his eyebrows, "Different version?"

"Look, I just want to ask the doc here some questions, fix this, and go home."

"That's all we want to do." I pointed to the vest around Blu's neck.

"Yours stopped working, too?

"Am I essential to all this or can I..."

Strawberry barked, "Stay."

"Hey, hey, let's just all sit here, have a mocha and talk. This could be quick. We want the same thing you do."

"Excuse me?" a girl with pink hair in a Starbucks uniform tapped me on the shoulder. Thinking back, this was brave. "There's a table for eight on the patio to the side. Can I put this on your bill?"

She pointed to the hole in the door.

I looked at Albio, "Alan Biolenski?"

He sighed.

"So, you three are from the future?" The doctor pointed at me, Thunderdome, and Strawberry. "And where are the rest of you from?"

Davina shook his hand politely. "We're from Peoria. It's a hundred-and-seventy miles away. It's nice to meet you. We've heard great things."

Dr. Ron shook her hand. He was an erudite if baby-faced black man in a well-kept dark blue suit. He looked as though he had just gotten a haircut for his lecture. "That's a great town. Very nice to meet you."

"So, just a few days ago, all of these seemed to stop working, all at the same time."

"Oh my," he seemed to understand easily.

"And if we can't travel we're like…" and I made a gesture with my fingers and mouth.

"Eating?"

"No, the other thing, with the dick and mouth and stuff. Facefucked."

"I don't know if I can be any help. I've theorized, but never really had the funding to build a time travel device." He pointed to Blu's vest around her neck, "If I can ask, how much do they cost?"

"Well, adjusted for money in this time, it's about eight-hundred-thousand dollars each, but if you build them in bulk, you get efficiencies. Mine has a translator, too, since I don't speak English."

"Really. A real universal translator? Can I see?" he reached over.

Strawberry was getting impatient, "So, now you're a NeuroScientist?"

"Hey, Strawberry. I think he's allowed to be interested in more than one scientific field."

"My name is Ayjay." He looked down. He seemed to lack the self-awareness to know he was shaped like a strawberry. "I'm sorry doctor, sir. It's been a hard couple of days."

The doctor put his hand on his shoulder. Despite everything, he was a giver. A nurturer. "It's going to be ok." He looked down at the vest on the table. "It's beautiful. No doubt. I can see what it's doing. Coherent light to swirl spacetime and initiate a reaction that folds it. It makes sense. And it's what I would do. Up until now, you say they worked?"

"Because of you," Davi interjected.

Albio walked back with a tray of drinks and began the complex task of getting each to their assigned owner. Everybody's name was spelled correctly except for Sean's.

"How goes it?"

"Well, the Doctor thinks they should work. But they don't"

Doctor Ron showed Albio, "This ring of lasers creates an intense and continuous rotating beam of light that is able to manipulate gravity. It mimics the spacetime-distorting effects of a black hole. Technically, according to my research, you can send information, objects, etc. back, but you can only send it back to the point where you started operating the device."

"But that's not how yours works," he pointed to the vest.

"It's mostly how all of ours work. But we solved the problem of being able to go back beyond the machine inception point. They broke the rules and sent a beacon way back in time. That's now the new machine inception point for all time travel devices."

Davina perked up, "You didn't tell us that."

Los cut in. "So, there is a machine in the far past that every time machine has to kind of click with in order to work?"

The doctor looked at me, "If that artificial inception point were to go down, they would all stop working, wouldn't they?"

"Fuck," Ayjay Berry put his head in his hands, "It's in the past. Way back. There's nothing we can do."

If it's the inception beacon it's not my fault. I admit, that made me feel worse. Not my fault = I can't fix it.

"That's just my take," Dr. Ron looked at Albio. "Can I see that?"

"Oh, the gun, sure." He handed it to him.

Dr. Ron gingerly looked at the gun, studying it.

I looked over the cheap plastic table at The Big Berry.

"You're here to stop something called the Nuclear Demon? What is that?"

"Same as you?"

"No, we're on the Mitchel Wagner thing."

He waved, "That's resolved. That was nothing. This is the end of all timelines. It happens about twenty years after me."

"We don't know. We don't go there anymore. The first people we sent disappeared and sent a symbol back. Like a nuclear symbol with a pentagram in it."

Dr. Ron was suddenly not so interested in the laser gun.

"So, a nuclear symbol with a star in it?"

"Yeah, with kind of atomic particles."

The doctor fished in his pocket. He placed a card on the table. "Did it look like this?"

The bright white symbol floating on a blue bed looked exactly like what he described.

I turned the card over.

"EntheoGen | Unlock the Future."

Davi read the rest. "Offices in Chicago, Peoria, Pennsylvania, and New York."

Dr. Ron looked up apologetically, "They're the sponsors for my lecture."

"Fuck this," StrawberryJay jumped up and grabbed the gun in the center of the table and pointed it at me. Albio moved first and tried to cover me. Then he...

That's just it. I have no idea what Ayjay was about to do next.

Because a version of me appeared in a black t-shirt, grabbed him from behind and shouted, "Like This."

As she disappeared, I made note that my voice sounded tinier and higher listening to it from elsewhere. Does everyone hate their own voice?

The gun clatterred to the floor.

Blu stared into the space where they were a second ago. "That was pretty fucking rude."

And Dr. Ronald Mallett, who had spent his whole life trying to master time travel so he could save the father he loved, had just seen, with his own two eyes, the very first proof that time travel was real.

He looked up and smiled.

Chapter Eight:

Slapping is Hot

"Do you folks have bladder problems?"

"Sorry about that, sir. You'll stop smelling anything at all shortly." Blu showed him to the counter.

"Well, hopefully that happens soon." Dr. Ron was definitely not enjoying the inside of the RV.

"I don't miss smelling at all, really," Albio found a place for him to sit.

"Isn't it bad for the timeline for you to show me things? What if this makes whatever I invent happen faster?"

"Yeah, no one cares. We just went over this. It will be a different timeline if you make enough changes. And the universe is fine with that."

"So, you aren't changing things in your timeline? So why do you come back at all?"

"If I can, let me use this example. You could go back and warn your dad to get a heart test."

"Ok." The Dr. looked immersed.

"And if it worked and he lived longer, that would be enough of a change to create a new timeline."

"So, it's hopeless?"

"No, not at all. Let's say you do that. And a version of you from this timeline does it, and this one, etc. Now, maybe the number of timelines where your dad is alive starts to grow."

"Ok, like more branches?"

"Exactly, but we're using a stream metaphor. These timelines are all really close. So, just like a bunch of distributaries coming off a stream, if they are close enough, they eventually 'try' to merge again."

Los jumped in, "There are forces that want them to come together and become, like, a confluence. They merge. And that may start to affect the other streams. Once the confluence gains enough energy."

Blu continued, "And then you may start remembering, for example, that your dad lived a little longer, or he was healthier, or something."

Albio asked, "This doesn't sound very accurate or scientific. Exact."

I sat on the long couch along the wall of the RV. "You know the really accurate stuff you see all the time, like clocks and rulers and straight lines and perfect circles and her head?" I pointed to Blu, "We made them up. Humans. We invented them."

Dr. Ron continued, "She's right. The best we get is a statistical universe which veers toward accuracy when the numbers get big enough."

Sean and Davi opened the door to the RV and stepped in. Sean threw a bag at me. Davi said, "Happy birthday."

It was a black t-shirt. Sean pointed at the shirt.

"This is how you fucking manifest."

I appreciated that. I pulled off the Quantum Leap shirt and tossed it on the chair, sliding the black shirt over my head. I then realized I had just flashed the father of modern time travel, and I felt kind of good about that. He deserved some titties.

Blu asked the Dr. "Can you think of any way that this combination of drugs could do the same thing as the time vests?"

"Well," Dr. Ron was trying to open his mind here. "Ok, swirling light stirs up spacetime as it impacts with gravity. But that's a real effect, not just a perception."

"And the drugs alter our perceptions, not reality."

"But our perceptions are part of how the universe sees itself."

Davi jumped in, "I love that."

Albio not so much, "That seems really new agey and unscientific."

"When you use the vest, what do you see?" the Dr. asked.

It felt strange telling HIM this. "Um, we see the lights swirl. And we can see the holes it makes. You step into one."

"And when you did it before using drugs?"

"I saw something really similar. The lights just seemed different. Louder."

Blue wrinkled her forehead, "I don't know what that means."

"Like they were just different lights."

Davina was thinking. "What if light is always swirling like that, stirring spacetime? And these devices and tools let us see the swirls so we can step into them and travel."

"What are these kinds of photons that we aren't seeing until we're high?" The Doctor was curious.

Sean was looking at his phone. "We can find out. I got a hotel room."

He put his phone back in his pocket with a flourish. "You guys want to go get ripped?"

The room was fairly big with two massive beds in the center and a little office type area and kitchenette. It honestly wasn't much smaller than my apartment where I came from. It was cleaner, though.

As soon as we walked through the door, I grabbed Albio and dragged him into the bathroom. I shut the door and kissed him hard.

"What was that for?" he asked, smiling.

I slapped him across the face.

"You tried to jump in front of a laser gun for me. What the fuck were you thinking?"

"He wasn't going to - "

"Yes, he was going to shoot me."

"Well, he didn't."

"Don't ever fucking do it again."

"Because you like me?"

"I like parts of you, sexually. A lot of you is annoying. Most of the stuff in the neck and head area is annoying." I kissed him harder. I slapped him, "Don't fucking do it."

He picked me up by the ass as I slapped him a few more times, harder. It seemed to be kinda working for him, honestly. He was breathing harder. He slid me on to the sink, far more substantial than the last one, and pulled my jeans off. I steadied myself with my left hand. I leaned into him, feeling down with my right hand, grabbing his cock and angling it into me. I was already wet, which forced me to consider that the slapping may have been working for me, too.

"Fuck," he whispered. "I love this much more advanced human pussy."

"It's a very tech forward cunt, caveman."

"I like it." He moved back and forth, and I put my head into the warm area of his neck and wrapped my arms tight around the stupid fucking idiot who tried to jump in front of a gun for me.

And he felt so good.

We walked out and saw that the Dr. was gone. "Where Dr. Ron go, human owner?"

I pet him on the head and shrugged.

Los looked apologetic. "I explained to him what happened last time and he said to take good notes and he split."

Davi took her shirt off. "That's too bad." She threw the shirt behind the bed. Los handed me the joint. It looked like we would have to catch up. She was pretty far ahead of us.

Davi put on "Grooveline" by HeatWave and started to dance. Her hands were in the waistband of her skirt as she danced to make it easier to take off. She was fucking beautiful, not as dark as me, but smooth and radiant and covered everywhere with little freckles like stars on an inverted space field. Her nipples were perfectly round and twice as dark as the rest of her, hard and pointing out in front of her as she danced.

Get this train, know you'll be glad you came

Hit the track, party hard there and back

Leave your worries behind

'Cause rain, shine, won't mind

We're ridin' on the groove line tonight

Yeah, Dr. Ron was going to regret missing this.

"So, this is the same thing?" I asked, taking a hit.

"It's basically the same." Los came up close and I blew smoke into his mouth. He inhaled and reached down, tweaking my bare ass. I was still wearing only the black shirt that Sean had gotten for me. Los spun me around and laughed and dipped me.

He always seemed to have the exact same amount of five o'clock shadow. But today, it looked a little darker. I wondered where he came from. He seemed Colombian or maybe Dominican. He seemed swarthy and alive, like a pirate. Dangerous. This was always such a thick contrast with Sean who was scraggily handsome in a boyish and pure way. Sean was the angel to Los' little devil.

I plopped down onto the bed next to Albio and watched Los drop to his knees in front of me. He looked up at me like a knowing puppy dog and I pulled his head between my legs and made a show of crushing his head while he licked at me. His hands on my ass felt stable, grounding.

What the hell. I was feeling pretty good already. Let's hear it for FourStar. In my head, I said, "Get to work, little pirate hippie," and that made me laugh out loud.

I handed the joint to Albio and he took a deep hit. He laid back in the bed and turned to look up at me, rubbing the small of my back.

Davi climbed on top of him, kissing him and rubbing her tits on him in rhythm with the music.

I watched as they slowly shifted positions, kissing each other's bodies, until her pussy was right over his mouth and her face could bury itself between his legs. The hair between her legs was jet black and tightly curled, making her belly look warm and soft.

He passed the joint to her and she inhaled, holding it in as she slid his dick into her mouth, slowly. She turned her eyes to the side and looked at me as she handed the blunt back to me. She was pushing down harder now, riding Albio's face. I reached over to hold his hand and he held on tightly.

I laid back, still with my legs spread. Los' mouth was wet and soft between them. Blu moved over to the side of the bed. She was just wearing her vest.

"One for us," and she passed the joint to me. "And one for later, "she dropped one into her vest pocket.

I turned my head to look at her. That just seemed hilarious to me.

"I like the little dimples in your back when you bend over."

She smiled, "Oh, really? What brings this up now?"

I laughed, "You were telling me all the things I could make fun of you for. I wanted to tell you what I liked."

"Oh, you do." She put her lips on mine and they were soft and pliant. I kissed her. "You must be super high already." She opened her mouth and kissed me properly, greedy, wet.

"I like your little titties. They are fun-sized. "I pulled her up a little to slip each nipple in my mouth. She closed her eyes and inhaled when I played my tongue and teeth lightly over each nipple. I could tell they were sensitive.

"Do you like them both?"

"I like this one. The other one could be terrible. Let me see."

I pulled at her and she put the other one in my mouth, holding my head with her hand while she played with my belly with the other one. She pressed down a little right over the spot where Los' fingers were edging me as he licked. I sucked in air.

"You taste good. I wish I could still smell anything anymore."

She kissed me and her open mouth felt endless. She grabbed the joint and we blew smoke into each other's mouths. I could feel Albio's hand while he slowly moved inside Davina's mouth over and over. I squeezed his hand hard.

"I like watching you get fucked like a whore by my boyfriend," I said loud enough for him to hear the 'B' word.

"Oh, so he's your boyfriend now. Not just a pet?"

My belly bounced while I laughed. "Oh, he's still a beloved pet. But he also almost got a hole blown in his head for me today, so…"

"And that's the way to your heart?"

"Yeah. Self-immolation is my love language."

I could feel myself starting to cum, the more Los teased me with his tongue and fingers. I leaned into Blu and yanked her back hard.

I could see out of the corner of my eye that Albio had rolled over on top of Davina and was slowly riding her pussy. I grabbed Blu by the waist and pulled her on top of me, too. She tried not to crush me, but I wrapped my hands around her waist and wouldn't let her up.

I put both my hands on hers and held them behind her while I pushed my tongue up her ass as hard as I could. She started to moan and rock back and forth. I wondered if I could get her off this way and I started digging deeper, sucking her ass, feeling her pussy juices on my face and neck. I was getting closer to cuming and something about the entire thing made me feel alive.

Like I was right where I needed to be. Where the universe needed me to be. I wanted this to go on.

I could feel her start to cum and I tried to hold off myself until she was there so we could do it together. She was warm and open and soft and so pliable. I pulled harder at her hands behind her, pulling her down and I could tell that she liked it. Suddenly, I felt a tiny warm flow of liquid on my neck from her pussy and felt her ass constrict as we both came at the same time.

The lights had been intensifying the entire time, building and threatening to force my eyes closed.

The light began to throb and I counted the beats. On the desk, a tiny drummer counted it off with his sticks. It was a rhythm and it sucked me in. He shook his head along to the beat as the lights shimmered. Tiny drummer began playing, and then, with his tiny left boot, kicked the TV off the desk. He pointed his sticks at me and said, in rhythm, "Don't count it out, baby, just listen."

As I felt everything from the past day melt, I opened my eyes wider and the drummer started falling. The desk followed and everything else, until the entire room fell away, rhythmically. I laid there breathing hard while Blu tapped my stomach. I looked at her face as she slid off mine. Her eyes moved around the room.

We were surrounded by a group of clowns in an outdoor gazebo. Everything sounded and felt familiar. I listened.

We were at the convention.

I should stop here for a second and sort of break these drugs down and what they do. If you aren't a massive drug guy, some of this may sound weird.

Five things about what these drugs CAN do:

1. Altered perception of time

Ironically, each of these drugs, Marijuana, Ketamine, Ecstasy, and LSD all create a completely fucked up perception of time and its passage. One of the reasons this happens is because many of the brain areas involved in timing and recognition of the passage of time are also responsible for emotional processing. Because the brain is thrifty as shit and likes to reuse areas kind of like your grandma using old cookie tins for sewing kits, when these areas have to try to process emotion and also do their job processing time, shit can get distorted. This is why you never got home on time when you were a kid having fun at a party. In fact, much of the high you get from some of these drugs is emotion taking over these areas and distorting time. Time distortion alone can get you high.

2. Visual effects

You can see all sorts of strange lighting and shifting visuals. These visual effects are thought to result from interaction with the brain's sensory processing regions. Remember, your brain is doing most of the seeing. Your eyes are upside down, even, delivering an inverted image. Your brain flips it, adjusts it, sets the colors, it even fills in areas that are missing so you don't notice. Your brain does way more seeing than your eyes do. It's not just interpreting. It's actually seeing. Your brain is very invested in visuals. It processes them first, before a lot of other sensory input. So this is a big deal.

3. Emotional intensity

Drugs like Ecstacy can heighten emotional intensity and create new intimate experiential bonds in places where none existed before.

They can easily tie your experience with a person into a dopamine high that can create an engram in your head, making that connection more significant in a short period of time. If this sounds like your brain is giving you Stockholm Syndrome, it's because it is. This plasticity of experience is also found in other drugs, like Ketamine, where focusing on the positive experiences with someone, even if few, can lock in magical emotional highs that reconstruct experiences in your head from then on. Often it's the job of the user to drive the car into a positive place, but after that, the drug can take over and amplify it, driving it to the party or off the cliff.

4, Hallucinations

Many drugs contribute to the body's heightened levels of dopamine. That's why people do them. In schizophrenics, there is evidence that very high levels of dopamine in the limbic system can play a major role in the development of hallucinations and delusions. Antipsychotic medications, which block central dopamine activity, alleviate the hallucinations of psychosis. But because they work this way, they cut the user off from the dopamine feelings, which then makes them feel like shit. You can think of dopamine as 'the magic in your brain.' Imagine being schizophrenic and taking medication that makes you feel like all the magic is gone? It doesn't matter if your dog isn't telling you to kill that Emily girl because now, you just want to kill everyone.

5. Perceived happiness

There are four chemicals in your brain that create the positive emotions that you end up feeling: dopamine, oxytocin, serotonin, and endorphins. We can refer to these as D.O.S.E. if we want to be cute. Many drugs aspire to manipulate these chemicals in various configurations to create kinds of wellness or happiness. That's the plan, anyway.

"So, at what point are we time traveling and what point are we just planning drug fueled orgies?"

"It can't be both?"

"We probably need a goal?"

"That's a great question for after I do this."

I took a big bite out of the massive strawberry funnel cake, spilling a little onto the front of the black shirt, the only clothing I was wearing. Blu was wearing her vest and a pair of boots I hadn't noticed earlier. That would have turned me on like a motherfucker. It was a pretty good look. Stomp here, bitch.

Luckily, people at the convention were not unfamiliar with a few naked time travelers. Hell, some of the timelines actually had large nudist communities. I felt like I needed shoes at least, though. The ground was sticky.

"I think the question is, are you having fun?"

"I was hoping to get back to my own time at some point. Or at least learn some words in English so I can take this off."

"Do you know the word, 'snowglobe'?"

"Ha. Hilarious."

"Omigod. You can't even be snotty with me now. You fucking like me."

"I like you a little bit until I come down from that orgasm." She glowered at me and made a motion with her fingers. "A little bit."

"I'll take it."

"What are we doing?"

"Well, I'm discovering a new way to travel so that I can do the job I was meant to do and then attend to this Nuclear Demon thing. Along the way it looks like I'm going to get super high, bitches."

"I wish I were more like you. You never stop and wonder if this is the right path. You just move forward."

"Oh, my little hoofd als een kers. It's all a giant ride and we have to be prepared to not throwup before the end." I grabbed her cheeks and smushed them a little, kissing her on the lips.

Without moving, "Did you learn how to say 'Head like a cherry' in Dutch just to annoy me."

And I had.

"Do you see yourself here anywhere?"

She looked around, "No. I don't remember any of the times I was here. You remember your last time. Do you know where you are?"

I looked through my memory. I had a general idea of where I was with Albio this last time. But if this was a test, what we really needed to do was to get back.

I looked past her to the "FreeJack Jack and Coke shop," which was practically empty. People hated that movie. The cast was good. The idea wasn't bad. I don't know what fucking happened. We forget that Hannah Waddingham was in that, before she was prime minister.

"Do you still have that joint?"

She fished in her vest pocket and pulled it out.

"Cool. Let's go challenge the dress code of this fucking Michelin starred establishment."

"Jesus, it's quiet in here."

"You miss the clowns. I knew it"

"If they didn't travel in packs, it wouldn't be so weird."

We moved to the darkened back with a big plush couch. On the way back, I flicked on some lights and tried to point the ones that were already on.

"We need some lighting."

I sat cross legged and held out my hands. Cherryhead sat right across and did the same, giving me her hands. I helped them both in one hand while I lit the joint and breathed in. The familiar taste already kickstarted some big feelings. I could feel Blu's heartbeat in my hands and I concentrated on it. I looked at her and passed the joint to her. She smiled that weird little Asian smile she does and inhaled.

I noticed how pretty her eyes were. I looked deeply into them. The lights I had pointed toward us were flashing in her eyes now, strobing every time she moved her head slightly. Each movement seemed to kick up more light, which flowed like jelly around her. I remembered how it felt kissing her and getting her off, and how satisfying it was feeling her cum with my mouth. I smiled thinking that we were here together and she was mine for a while.

I thought about Blu growing up, her first twenty or so years, in the wrong body, looking like, having to act like a boy. And then, one day she opened up like a chrysalis and burst out like a butterfly. I imagined the sound of her flying, the butterfly wings flapping. I imagined her happy for the first time.

I imagined her laughing for the first time as herself.

I inhaled the smoke and thought about a universe that lets us create like that. Giving someone life is creating life. Letting someone fly is inventing flight over and over again. She looked at me and I saw in her eyes that she was opening up to me. I felt the butterfly wings behind her before I saw them. And each time they flapped, there was a woosh and a gelatin thick swirl of lights. I opened my eyes wider as the whooshes got faster. The light took me in, and then a hole broke in the center of it. It widened and dissolved.

And we were back in the room. Sitting on the bed together. The room was darkened, but I could still see her. I leaned over and we kissed.

And the screaming started.

"Holy fuck." Albio slammed into us on the bed, fully dressed. He held the two of us and dug his face into my neck. Davina and Sean and Los came after. I could tell Davina had been crying. She grabbed my face and kissed me.

"It's been over an hour."

'I don't know how long we were gone in our time."

Blu thought, "Well, it took us about twenty minutes to get away from the clowns, we waited in line for about fifteen minutes at the Time Tunnel funnel cake shop, then about twenty minutes of walking around before we tried to get back."

I figured that was close. "Ok, so we were gone in real time, relationally. We didn't return right to our origin. That's good to know."

"I can't believe this fucking works," Albio sat back, relieved.

"I think there's an emotional trigger to it."

Sean was interested, "Like you have to be feeling a certain way for it to work?"

"Yeah. I've traveled three times so far. Each time, I had a kind of feeling." I turned to Blu, "What did you feel?"

"Ok, the first time, from here to the convention, I was thinking about how I wanted this to go on forever. I was just feeling like it was all good, no matter what part of me I listened to. And how long it's been since I felt that."

"Right. And the second time?"

"I was looking at you and thinking that we were a team, and that this is-"

"Where I belonged," we both finished at the same time.

"So you felt that?"

"Yes, I felt like I belonged in the universe, and it was capable of making me feel like that. And you. And it was open to us being in it."

Davina added, "You were grateful?"

"It was bigger than that. I was awed."

"Awe. That is the feeling?"

"Maybe. Awe and intimacy. Bigness and smallness. I felt in the presence of immensity, but not alone. Loved. A part of it."

Sean was looking at his phone. "Prayer is expressing awe and intimacy with God, who is the universe."

I looked around at everyone.

"Fuck."

Chapter Nine:

Deep Dive: The Breakfast Buffet

If you time travel, and I recommend it, it's fun, definitely do it, try to hit up as many breakfast buffets as you can. The breakfast buffet is essentially the most extraordinary invention the human race has ever made, no lie. This is where eternity begins. Here.

That is my hottest of takes on that.

And the scrambled eggs here are made with real eggs. Cray. Who does that?

"To get back, we didn't have to have sex or even watch each other have sex."

"I think we just focused on each other as the sort of 'avatar' of the universe," Blu finished.

I held up a sausage and showed it to her. "Look. It's your people. Mommy." She grabbed it and chucked it in her mouth.

Albio was intrigued. "So, just sort of thinking of the other one as a beautiful extension of a beautiful universe?"

"I think so." I had placed ten pieces of bacon on my plate and I slid one in my mouth hoping no one would notice.

"Oh, Lord, you are so very big..." Recited Sean.

Albio looked at him. "That's from..."

"Yes, Monty Python."

"Are we freaked out at all by the fact that all of this seems to be taking a turn toward the religious? And what's a Nuclear Demon?" Davi looked concerned.

I spoke up, "I automatically assume that when the conversation turns to religion, it's metaphorical. The universe basically IS god. I sometimes have a hard time distinguishing between what is anthropomorphizing and what is just noticing."

"Isn't the demonic part just the pentagram in this logo?"

"What does EntheoGen do?" asked Davi.

"According to the card, they unlock the future."

"So, who locked it in the first place?"

Sean read from his phone, "EntheoGen. Noun. A chemical substance, typically of plant origin, that is ingested to produce a nonordinary state of consciousness for religious or spiritual purposes."

I stared at him. "Well, that's a bit on the nose."

Davi countered, "You know, if I didn't have a cow tossed at me like two days ago, I would think that was overly on point."

"Right?"

"We'll figure it out when we get there." Blu ate one more of her own people. Silent scream.

"We will." I snuck another bacon. Fuck that pig in all his parts.

Davi asked first, "To EntheoGen?"

"Well, you guys don't have to, but it does seem like dark mysteries of the moon over here and I need to."

"I'm in," Albio started. "I think I'm fired anyway."

Nosferatu Barbie looked up. "Something is bugging me." It occurred to me that 'Nosferatu Barbie' was too good not to say out loud.

Davi waved her arms, "Most all of this is bothering me."

"What's bugging you, Nosferatu Barbie?"

That was better. It did sound good out loud.

She rolled her eyes, "Question one."

"Ok. I'm following."

Los was trying to stab some grapes with a fork. "What is question one?"

I waved to Blu and she continued, "When you do this thing that we do, if you're very good, you end up in a different timeline. If you get stuck, you end up in a different timeline. If your equipment malfunctions, you end up in a different timeline. Any of a number of things happen, you end up in a different timeline. And disgruntled people with time travel technology can fuck you up."

"No doubt." One more bacon.

"So the very first question they ask any of us, and the thing they look for is important."

"It's question one."

Davi was curious, "Ok, so what is it?"

"Can you enjoy yourself anywhere you are?"

"Definitely," Sean had built a pancake mountain and was playing with a possible syrup waterfall. My concern was deep soil erosion. "That makes sense."

"See? He'd do well." Just maybe not as an architect.

Los was kicking grapes at Albio now, who was catching them with his mouth.

"Them, too."

"No matter where you are and where you end up, they want to know you're going to have a good life. You're going to thrive, and sometimes maybe be cool with just staying somewhere, burning your equipment, staying out of the way of history, and having fun."

"That's crazy. Wow. Can you say that this way?" Albio was now trying to get a grape in my mouth like a little football. The team failure on this was not on the catcher side. You shouldn't be able to pronounce a kicker's last name, even I knew this. He sucked.

"We're selected to be people who enjoy ourselves."

"Which you think doesn't describe the Strawberry?"

"No, not even a little." Blu was pleased with herself for stealing a bacon from my plate, but I don't forget shit like that. Not even at the Buffet.

Davi cocked her head, "So you think he's lying?"

I looked at Blu, "I agree with boob head. He doesn't feel like one of us."

Albio abandoned his kicking career young, "So what do we do with this information?"

I thought for a second, "Let's just not automatically think we have the same goals." I finished the last bacon.

I looked over at Los now, who had fallen asleep into his plate of fruit.

"Assuming other me ever brings him back and this guy ever wakes up."

Intermission:

The Adventures of Carlos

Scene: Audience sees Blu carry Kerys from the front of the RV

"Yeah, I'm going to find a human bed for your owner."

(Audience laughs)

She passes Carlos and Sean, "Hey, guys, is the back bedroom free?"

Sean looks up, "Oh, Davi's in bed, but there's room. Whatcha got there?"

"You like? I just carry around human girls as an accessory. She's like a little purse."

Sean smiled, "Well, carry on."

(Rousing laughter)

"What are you guys up to?"

Carlos stood tall, "We are perfecting this blend."

Blu saluted and continued to the back, "Well, you carry on, too."

(Audience applauds. Blu exits)

Sean waved his hand. "All right, This is FourStar. Beautiful blend, great aroma, proven time travel effects, takes some time to kick in. Good stuff."

Carlos nodded as Sean continued, "Here will be the new blend. Just as tasty with just as much kick. Faster on the way up, faster on the way down. For the time traveler who has work to do."

Carlos was on board. "Got it. We need controllability and speed."

"Good, what do we got?"

"Trial one," Carlos read from a tiny clipboard and pulled out a joint, "Adderall."

Sean took a hit, "Sweet, For when you want to get there fast and have a term paper to finish"

"Cheers." Carlos took a hit, too.

(We see them smoke casually. As the camera pans backwards, there is a giant biblically angelic creature with his head in flames standing behind Sean, visible to Carlos. He looks up and squints. The creature makes a motion with his finger and mouth shushing him as the flame on his head lights the roof of the RV on fire.)

Sean looks approvingly, "I like."

(Carlos takes the joint from Sean's hand and tosses it in the sink, running the water.)

"Or not." Sean takes a deep breath. "Let's see what else we got."

Carlos pulls the page of the clipboard off and recites. "Trial two, cocaine." He hands the joint to Sean.

Sean picks up approvingly, "Ah, yes, the choice of Disco Dancers, Show Girls, and Wall Street Giants. Let's see."

(The two take a hit.)

(The audience makes a sound, ooooh, wondering what will happen this time.)

(Carlos hears a sound building. He looks to one side and hears a throbbing electric beat.)

(As he looks around, he realizes that the interior of the RV is filling with smoke. Panicked, he grabs the fire extinguisher. He turned around and he's in a club. On stage is him in a beautiful dress. The version of him onstage begins to sing.)

Ooh, it's so good, it's so good

It's so good, it's so good

It's so good

Ooh, I'm in love, I'm in love

I'm in love, I'm in love

I'm in love

(Carlos looks down and he sees that his clothes have changed. He's in a white suit and he feels alive. He moves toward the stage.)

Ooh, I feel love, I feel love

I feel love, I feel love

I feel love

I feel love

I feel love

I feel love

(He dances for a few moments with people he sees along the way on his way to the stage. As he steps up, the version of him singing on stage looks at him seductively.)

Ooh, fall and free, fall and free

Fall and free, fall and free

Fall and free

Ooh, you and me, you and me

You and me, you and me

You and me

(He steps on stage and begins dancing with the seductive songstress, spinning her on the stage. He dips himself and tweaks his ass.)

Ooh, I feel love, I feel love

I feel love, I feel love

I feel love

(The camera moves around him in circles as he dances and the lights become hypnotic and vibrant, swirling, moving. Everything spins faster until it finally slows and pulls away.)

Carlos is standing back in the RV, smiling, holding the joint. Sean is asleep on the couch a few feet away. He takes a deep breath and reaches for the clipboard, tossing the joint into the sink.

(Carlos tries again. He begins running through iterations.)

(Scene: Carlos stands in the RV surrounded by Bedtime Bear, Birthday Bear, Cheer Bear, Friend Bear, and Funshine Bear, each one of which has a joint of their own. He writes down their responses on the clipboard and each one disappears one at a time, like a popped soap bubble. Sean sleeps through it all.)

(Scene: Carlos rips off a page from the clipboard and tries a new blend, lighting it up. He tries to pass it to Sean who is still asleep. He shrugs and takes another hit. The light begins to swirl and another version of him steps out of it. He takes the joint and the two of them smoke together.)

(Scene: Two versions of Carlos work with a tiny distillery in the center of the table. The camera pans down. There is a tiny version of Carlos floating in the water. They scramble to get him out. It spills on the table and he slides out. He is naked. He looks up and gives them a thumbs up. They return the thumbs up.)

(Scene: Carlos ruffles the hair of the other Carlos and he goes to leave through a light swirling portal. The first Carlos stops him and points to himself. They both nod and laugh a little. The audience laughs. First Carlos goes through the portal. The audience says "awwwwww." Carlos clearly misses himself.)

(Scene: Carlos is smoking, by himself. The RV starts to shake. The door opens and a giant duck pushes its head through the door. A group of smaller Dinosaur Ducks follow and jump up on the table. Carlos swats them away and tosses the joint in the sink, running the water.)

(Scene: Sean is still sleeping. Carlos smokes a joint and walks though a light portal. The same portal appears behind the table and he emerges from that seconds later. His beard is now a bit longer. He runs his hands through his hair and holds the joint up, inspecting it. He makes a mark on the clipboard and sets it down, moving to where Sean sleeps and sitting on the ground in front of him and closing his eyes. Sean wraps his arm around him and they sleep.)

(Audience applauds and laughs)

"So, you put a little what in the last one?"

Sean walked ahead a bit and turned around, "Well, we tried a bunch of things, and the one that worked the best, the one that sped up the process was meth."

Blue sounded concerned, "So I had crystal meth?"

"Well, technically, it was liquid. Liquid meth."

"That's much better, thank you."

EntheoGen was walking distance, if you enjoyed a long walk. And a lively conversation about the suite of drugs you had recently ingested. This was like if you made the tv show "Weeds" have unprotected sex with "The Brady Bunch" and waited for a new little show to pop out.

"Did the process seem faster this time?"

"It did, he's right. It felt more stable and fast." I offered.

"So, wait, did you guys travel when you tested it?" Davi was fascinated.

"He did," Sean pointed to Los. Los shrugged.

Albio put his arm around Los, "That's cool. You don't have to tell those fuckers anything."

I could see the EntheoGen sign. It really did look like a symbol for Nuclear Demon. There was something strangely familiar about it. I tried to think back. Whatever was happening, they seemed involved at least.

"Ok, I think we need to split up for this."

Blu stopped and looked at me, "I'm listening."

I looked over at Sean and Davi, "Do you guys have your locations on your phones tracked?"

Sean showed me his phone. "We always know where the other one is."

"Perfect. We can use that to find each other."

I adjusted Blu's vest.

"You take Fabio and the human ruffie and go in the front way, talk to the front desk, pretend you belong there, scout it out. I'll take the hot black chick and Elmo and we'll sneak in the back way and try to pretend I didn't just say 'the back way.'"

I saw some safety vests sitting near a construction site and helped myself to two of those. Handing them to Albio and Sean, "Here. you guys all match now."

Albio adjusted it, "Cool. Cosplay. What are we looking for?"

"I don't know. We're used to this. We look for triple As - 'Anomalous Activity or Artifacts.' Things, behaviors, whatever, that don't belong for any reason. If you find a triple A, you let me know. "

I looked at Albio and he patted his pocket. He still had the light gun. And I still had mine. That made me feel a little better.

Davi, Los and I made our way to the back of the building. Once we started, it would be a lot easier for the others. I assumed they would figure out what to do. I admit that this was always my thing, though, mindless destruction. I surveyed the situation. There was a loading dock with an electrical entry and what looked to be a massive transformer on a pole in back. There were no people there.

I pulled out the gun and severed one of the many lines leading to the transformer. It hung down the pole. Picking up a nearby stick, I grabbed the wire and draped it over the metal box that contained the electrical entry control for the door.

I stood back to survey my work.

I winked at Davi. "Boom," I shot the transformer. A wave of electricity ran down the wire and caused a mini explosion that popped the door open. All in all, it was unspectacular. I felt bad about that wink now.

"Damn."

Davi pointed. "The door is open. Good work."

I put the gun in my pocket.

"I was thinking bigger." The three of us moved into the doorway and tried to avoid being seen.

The hallway led to a boiler room in one direction, and off to the main building in the other. I wanted the boiler room.

We stepped inside and closed the door.

"I've been in this situation before. How to make as big a noise as possible and not actually do anything that hurts anyone."

I glared at them both.

"Because I'm not a psychopath."

Los cocked his head and looked, conjuring. "Water to steam is a sixteen-hundred to one pressure increase."

"I was thinking that, without the numbers." So, how to make that happen fast.

"What are we exactly trying to do?" Davi asked.

"Make. Noise."

Los pointed. "The center one." He walked over to the group of boilers. "We empty the ones on this side, around it. Now, they are inert and big enough to keep the blast from moving this way. We superheat the center one and it blows, exciting the other two by the outside wall, knocking out the wall to the alleyway."

"Big noise. No casualties. Big hole in EntheoGen."

Davi asked, "Ok, is that a retaining wall?"

"Don't be a buzzkill, DAVINA. Do you think that's a retaining wall?"

"I don't. There are a ton of columns. I mean, yeah, it's an outside wall, so..."

"Well, I'm inclined to buy it. This is literally the most words you've said since you fished me out of your pool, so..."

Los and Davi emptied the water out of the boilers nearest us. It poured onto the floor. Fuck your hot water, EntheoGen. Shower at home, bitches.

I motioned to them to move out into the hallway as I widened the lenses on my homemade light gun. I think I would name her Maggie. Pointing at the center boiler, I flashed it with Maggie for about thirty seconds to superheat the exterior. I heard a tiny groan and ran into the hallway.

It was magnificent. The entire hallway shook with the sound of the boom. Almost immediately, the sprinklers kicked in and alarms began to sound throughout the building.

We moved down the hallway. A few men in blue work shirts were running our way. I waved them off.

"We need you to get people out of here. We have to wait for the city to get here-it's their problem. Legal doesn't want anyone getting hurt. Got it?"

They nodded and ran back.

For future reference, I want to explain what I just said there. This is a tool that you can use, potentially, to get people to do what you want in any crisis situation. Are these the droids they're looking for? Who knows?

Five ways to make people do what you want in a crisis.

1. Be authoritative.

Your tone has to be effortlessly authoritative. You know what you are doing. When people are confused and confronted by someone who knows exactly what to do, it is their nature to listen and conform. Chaos is your friend if you keep calm.

2. Give them something exact to do.

"We need you to get people out of here." - People want to do SOMETHING in the middle of chaos. Give them a task, no matter how pointless. Now they are part of the winning team that knows what's up. And once on that team, it's hard, in their minds, to give up their team badge. And you don't want it. You NEED it.

3. Absolve them of blame.

"We have to wait for the city to get here-it's their problem."
Make sure they know that they aren't getting in trouble for
this. At this point, by helping, they are the heroes. In no way
will they be the bad guy. It frees their brains up to believe
you.

4, Give them a shared goal. Mention people they want to share a goal with.

"Legal doesn't want anyone getting hurt." They don't want
anyone getting hurt, either. And they REALLY want to be on
the same side as the Legal department. Who doesn't? Who
wants to be sued? No one has that kink.

5, Assert Authority like a motherfucker.

"Got it?" This basically says, "Did you hear me? I'm so
comfortable giving you an order that I want to treat you like a
child for a moment. And no, do not ask who I am."

Remember, in times of crisis, the world needs a leader. Be that leader.

Blu, Albio, and Sean stood by the front of the building.

Albio asked, "So, when do we go in?"

Blu looked around, "I think we'll know." She pointed to his vest.

Sean perked up, "Hey, since we're here waiting. Can I ask you a question?"

"Shoot."

"You said you were born male, but you are flawlessly female in every way,
if I can say."

Blu did a little curtsy, "You can say."

"In your time, how do they do it? Gender affirming stuff. Care. Surgery. Whatever?"

"Oh, it's not surgery. It's gene therapy. It took me a longer time than most to figure out who I was. That I was female."

"Flawlessly." Albio put his hand on her back and she smiled. He was the human ruffie.

"It's actually easier this way, male to female. Human bodies want to be female. Maleness is sort of an add-on. In my time, it's a pill. It can work both ways, though. Takes a day or two."

"One pill? A day or two?" Sean was amazed.

"Yep. Why are you so interested?"

Sean looked serious for maybe the first time.

"My brother. He's been... it's just been hard for him. Since he realized, and man, one pill. Do you realize how many people in our time would do anything for one of those pills?"

Blu moved over to Sean and put her arms around his waist. "You know what? When this is done, I'm gonna bring you back a fucking box of them. A huge box."

And that's when they heard the explosion. Suddenly people were running everywhere. Blu kissed Sean's forehead and started through the doors. They followed.

Blu walked confidently through the open reception area, where people were streaming to get out of the building. She stepped up to the pretty blonde receptionist, Albio and Sean right behind her. She put her hand on the phone to get her attention.

"Excuse me, I need you to keep these people moving out orderly. We're here from the city. Electric needs us downstairs before this happens again. Now."

We moved through the hallway under the chaos of the sprinklers. I was specifically looking for wider hallways, more opulent doors, things that would suggest wealth. People in charge liked to feel like people in charge at all times, and they rarely neglected the trappings of that wealth.

"They're in the building, moving toward us," Davina held up her phone, shielding it from the drizzle of water.

We made our way up the stairs, surrounded by people rushing down the stairwell.

"Keep moving, everyone. There are people on the main floor to assist you out."

Davina looked quizzically at me as if to say, "Are there?"

I shrugged back at her as if to say, "Who the fuck knows, you crazy bitch. I don't have eyes everywhere. What do I look like, a biblically accurate representation of Metatron? I'm just saying shit while running around a building. Cut me some slack."

There was a lot that shrug needed to communicate.

"There," I saw wide wooden doors. This is where I would be if I were the guy in charge. We approached the door and Maggie let us in.

"I don't know what I thought was going to be in that room, but I wasn't prepared for what was.

There was a row of tables - desks with seats. On them were dissected animals. Cats, dogs, smaller animals, a rabbit or two. And in cages, even more animals, many of them alive. Some looked as though they had been abused - brutalized.

There were posters, sketches, drawings all over the walls. Each one was worse than the one before. Decapitations, rapes, dictators, serial killers, monsters everywhere. There were charts on how to slit someone's throat, how to damage organs, even how to use rape and torture to get what you wanted.

And what did these people want?

Davi was overwhelmed. "Oh my god."

Los started opening the cages and pulling the animals out. He coaxed a rabbit out that had had its hind legs removed. He held it in his arms and looked at me, and I saw something in his eyes that made me want to kill some fuckers.

"What the fuck are they doing here?"

Davi ran to the door. "There are people coming."

We ducked behind the long partition that was used to split the room in two. If we were caught, we were caught. I didn't care. But we could see through the slats. I wasn't ready for what we saw.

Four boys ran in, ages ranging from twelve to about sixteen. A younger one trailed along afterward. They were laughing as they ran in to grab a few things from their desks. The oldest one looked up and my heart dropped. It almost seemed like he saw us. A younger boy punched him in the back and All five of them ran out, fighting.

We waited for another five minutes before any of us could even take a breath.

Davi whispered. "Was that what I think it was?"

I nodded. Five different kids.

Five different versions of Mitchel Wagner.

Chapter Ten:

Because Los is short for Carlos

Los met us back at the RV. He wasn't carrying the rabbit anymore. I assumed he'd put the poor thing out of its misery. He walked in and I wrapped my arms around him and kissed him hard. I kept it up until he kissed me back. We rocked back and forth for a minute and then I grabbed his hand.

Blu got up. She and Albio started pulling out the contents of their pockets. We had met up in the building before leaving EntheoGen but hadn't really had the chance to share much.

The contents of Albio, Blu, and Sean's pockets:

4 coherent light pistols

6 all access entry badges

3 USB hard drive sticks

1 disassembled battery for a time vest

2 Starbucks coupons

Assorted change

I sat on the couch and held Los' hand.

"So, what does this tell us?"

The bowling ball held up one of the guns, "They have people from the future," and then pointed to the battery, "and they took this apart. They don't know why the vests aren't working, either."

"Right," I countered. "I'm assuming the Starbucks coupons and the change are Sean's."

"Oops," Sean reached for the coupons, "Mine."

Albio picked up a quarter sized coin. "Not this one." He handed it to me. "Read."

It was from the future. After me. During my time, we certainly didn't have coins anymore, so that was confusing. On one side was a picture of Mitchel Wagner as an adult. On the other were the words, "eius unicum filium."

"I'm afraid to ask." I didn't know Latin. And I was honestly just afraid to ask.

Albio sighed and looked at Sean.

He said, "His only son."

"So, what, he's some kind of mythic Jesus figure in the future?"

I was considering that this entire adventure had started out very sci-fi and was now turning into a fucking C.S. Lewis Book. And I was going to need to get the fuck out of Narnia real soon.

Sean considered, "Well, this idea of God having to sacrifice his demigod type son - his chosen vessel - has some similarities with a lot of other religions from the past. Gods, even demons, have gained access to our plane of existence by sacrificing their own offspring."

"And the badges?"

Albio grabbed on, "Oh, so we can get back in if we need without blowing anything up. Nice, by the way."

"It's what I do." I shrugged.

Davi interjected, "So, they're grooming Mitchel Wagner to be some kind of monster so that he can be sacrificed?"

"Do you think they're just taking Mitchels from different timelines and training them up?" Blu asked.

"Don't tell me. He's eventually sacrificed to the Nuclear Demon?"

Albio started at me, "It fits."

"I don't want to play devil's advocate here, but this thing with Mitchel Wagner happens in about forty years. If he's alive. And robots took care of that here. The other thing, the end of all the timelines, that happens almost six-hundred years in the future. How are they connected?"

I looked around the room. That was a piece we didn't have solved.

Davi stood up. "Well, I know what I want to do?"

"What?"

Davi continued, "Here's my theory on time travel. You said that once you were in a timeline, you were just a regular person and we all had the same ability to impact the timeline."

Blue followed up, "Yes, that's true."

"So, I figure that the best way for me to make a better future is to do the right thing now, in the moment, and hope that it's the right thing for the timeline."

"That's fair."

"So, I don't think that this big company should be able to groom a bunch of kids to be monsters no matter what is going to happen potentially in what future. Or hurt people or animals to do it."

"Ok. agreed."

Davi was emboldened, 'So I'm going to do something about it."

"Yes." I stood up and started putting the badges together.

"So, what are we doing?" Albio asked.

I looked at the group.

"Oh, we're going to go steal a bunch of Mitchel Wagners."

The new adventures of Carlos and Max

Carlos walks down a sidestreet holding the black and white spotted rabbit. The rabbit seems calm, but is clearly in distress. He is missing his hind legs and seems resigned to die.

Carlos rocks him back and forth and pets him. He comes upon a park and walks in. There are one or two people moving around, but it's in the middle of a work day. Carlos and Max move to an uninhabited area of the park and he sits on a picnic bench, setting Max in front of him. He pets him and looks into his eyes.

Fishing in his shirt, he pulls out a joint. He takes a hit and holds it, while still petting Max. He scrunches the bunny's head up on top a bit, massaging it and Max's eyes close to slits.

It feels good.

Carlos takes another hit and blows it out.

Max inhales and shakes his head a bit. He looks more cartoonish.

One more hit and Carlos looks down. Max is a cartoon bunny. Carlos sees his own hands. He is also a cartoon. Smiling, he leans down to look into Max's eyes. The lights surround them and start to throb.

Max opens his mouth, his nose moving and twitching. He says excitedly,

"Hey, buddy, where we going?"

Carlos lifts him up and they step into the portal made by the light.

They find themselves in a cartoon version of the future. They are right outside a building with a big sign on it that says, "Pet Hospital". Under the title, in smaller letters it says, "Now's a good time to get that critter feeling fine." Carlos mouths that to Max, who perks up.

They go inside and sit in the waiting room. Some kids are playing with a jet pack. A cat is combing out its long lion's mane and tail. An alien lizard creature is seated right next to them. There is a bunch of noise. Max sits quietly on Carlos' lap.

The Nurse calls "Max" and Carlos gets up and goes through the doorway, back into the rooms.

Carlos kisses Max's head and sets him on the table. The doctor comes dancing in. She takes a pill and puts it in a tiny carrot. She makes a big deal out of handing the carrot to Max, who eats it nearly whole.

The Doctor continues to dance around the room, setting up a machine that points right at Max. Max leans back and sits, humanlike, on the table as the beam bathes him in light.

The doctor places a tiny pair of sunglasses on Max's face and he looks up, as though sunbathing.

His little hind legs grow back, almost too fast to see. He shakes them and points at them, showing them off to Carlos. Carlos is clearly very pleased and hugs the Doctor. Max hugs them both.

Carlos and Max are now both leaving the clinic on their own power. Max is hopping along next to him, showing off.

They walk down a futuristic street and see a ballerina in a window. Max stops and stares. Carlos reaches his cartoon hand inside the store and steals a leotard, handing it to max. They both look around suspiciously and hop away.

They walk further in the futuristic town, passing a place called "Bunnyland Dance." Looking inside, it seems to be a dance studio and home for rabbits. They look in the window to see many rabbits dancing.

A larger rabbit comes out to welcome them. Max and Carlos hug and shed a few tears. Max is clearly excited about the chance to dance, but will Miss Carlos.

Max goes inside to dance and Carlos watches through the window for a while. Max looks happy.

He slides down and sits on the ground, leaning up against the studio. Cartoon Carlos pulls a joint out and begins breathing it in. A portal appears next to him and he hops in slightly bunny-like.

Sean had driven the RV right up to the front of the building this time. Albio slid back in through the side door, "Ok. It's a different receptionist. We're good."

"Blue and I are going. Follow the plan."

Albio was positive, "I'm going, too."

"We're going to… Is this something you really want to do?"

"Yes, I'm definitely in. What they're doing is child abuse."

I looked at the other three, "Can you guys be getaway? When we need to go, we're going to need to go. Just remember what I said."

Davi shot back, "We're on it. 100%."

Carlos handed the three of us a few joints each.

"Let's not get arrested for misdemeanor drug possession before we do this."

Davi, Sean, and Los exited the RV, going to the side of the building while Albio, Blu, and I went back into the building the front way. We waited until one of the elevators was unattended and moved forward, sliding our badges and moving to the odd bank of elevators.

"USB stick three says that the seventh floor is where. But we know when."

Albio asked, "Ok, I don't know that part."

I shushed him as we tried to stay out of the way of the cameras in the elevator.

We stepped out on seven, "This is right down the hall from the classroom there." I pointed to the room with the wide doors. "Most of them will be here, but not all. It may be the best we can do."

Blu looked sneaky. "I may be able to do something about that."

We ducked into an empty room and I did a quick search for cameras. I turned and kissed Blu hard on the lips.

"Just getting in the right headspace."

Albio put up his hands, "So, what are we doing?"

Blu started, "We know one time when the place was in disarray and they weren't ready for us. And we're going back."

I sat cross legged on the floor. Blu sat next to me and Albio on the other side, in a circle. I pulled out a joint and lit it. I took a deep hit and held it in, passing it to Blu. I leaned over to Albio and breathed it onto his mouth. He held his breath as he took the joint from Blu. She leaned in and kissed me with her mouth wide open. I was starting to really like her lips.

She put her hand on my left breast and toyed with my nipple through my shirt. Albio handed me the joint back and slid his hand under Blu's skirt. She rearranged herself so he could slip his finger inside her. I kissed him and he pulled his finger out, placing it on my lips. We both licked it.

I took another hit and thought about how beautiful they both were. The lights in the room started to rise like smoke. Blu kneeled up and I put a few of my fingers in her, feeling her soft and wet in my hand. Albio and I took turns licking it and smoking while we kissed. I thumbed Blu's clit while playing with her, and she put her arms on our shoulders, leaning in. Her skirt was riding above her ass now, and she had put her head down, feeling it. I played with her, losing myself in Albio's mouth. As she got wetter, I tried to slide more of my hand inside, while making sure to give attention to her little button.

Blu started cumming in my hand, a sheen of slick wetness on my palm. I stared into Albio's eyes and we licked my hand together like animals. I put my other hand on the back of his head and jammed my tongue in his mouth.

As I finished, I looked down at Blu. Her skirt was up entirely, revealing her pussy with an elaborate tattoo of a strange foreign flower right above the clit. I could sense her lips pulling apart and a stream of light came out of her. She was everything. I wanted to tell her she was magnificent and beautiful and perfect, but then, just as i started, I realized she knew and we all were. I started to cry, thinking about how good she tasted and it made me want Albio in my mouth, too.

I put my hand in his lap and felt him hard as the light washed over us, spinning us. Everything felt in reach of my hands, like the world was just an RV where everything I wanted was something I could reach easily.

I wondered if this is what the universe was always trying to say to me, but I never listened.

I looked past Albio's beautiful face to a motivational poster on the wall with a cat hanging from a branch. The cat needed to let go, I thought. I wanted to tell him. Suddenly the cat looked at me.

"You can have everything in the world if you open your hands."

I smiled. The cat knew. The cat knew everything. He was going to be ok when that branch broke.

A hole opened in the light and I imagined we went through it.

A second later, it felt like the world had exploded. The alarms were blaring and the sprinklers were on, dousing us. Albio's eyes shot open. I forgot this would be his first time traveling.

"Oh my god," he looked around.

Blu moved over to the wall and opened a box. She looked at me and connected the wires from her translator. Suddenly her voice was being amplified across the building.

"MW class, please quietly meet in room 117."

"What's that room?" Albio asked.

"It's in an unused wing with a side exit. Your job is to get down there and put this lock on the door once they get in there. Then, move ahead again and get to the RV. If you can't move ahead, get back to the RV's south location. Stay out of sight, ok?"

"Got it." He kissed me and rushed off.

"Nice thinking there, voice of a nation. Ready to help me with the stragglers?"

Blu looked like she was having fun. There was a dark side to Question one. Were we hooligans? I suspected we were. "I am. Is it bad that I enjoy this method of travel way more?"

"Ha, well, you do actually owe me one now, so." I tried to get myself into a professional mindset as we slipped out into the familiar hallway. The five boys ran into the room. Looking past them, I could see a figure.

"Shit. Someone's with them."

"Who is it?"

"I can't see."

The lights flickered off and on. The figure shifted to one side. The boys came running out, as they did before, and he started to lead them down the hall. He turned to look back in our direction and I could see his face.

Looking a bit like a strawberry.

We waited until they passed and moved to the hallway. They were going into a side room. It must have been some sort of safety room. We waited until they were in and then glided down the hall. The door was locked, but easily opened when you lasered through the center lock mechanism. Inside the door was what looked like a waiting room. There was a hallway to one side, and we assumed that's where they had gone.

"That was him, right?"

"A version of him for sure. They all look alike."

"I do my hair differently in different timelines. I sort of like to be natural in this one."

"I'm usually bald. No idea why."

We could hear strawberry yelling at the Mitches. There was a laser blast.

"Shit." I jumped up. "We have to get back there. He's going to barbecue those little assholes."

"Wait," Blu held my arm. "If he knows we're here, he has all the cards right now. If we just pop up he shoots, right?"

I nodded. We rounded a corner and were right off of a large room. We could see him surrounded by the boys.

"Are you here to shoot me?" He yelled out.

I paused. "Sort of. But now we're all thinking that we should team up with you."

"What?"

"Well, you've got some Mitches. Actually we've got a shitload of Mitches. I'm sure we could work something out."

"No, you don't."

"We have a lot to trade. Mitches up the wazoo."

"What are you doing collecting Mitch Wagners?"

"The same thing you and EntheoGen are doing"

"No," he shot at my voice. It was too close for comfort, honestly. He was a good shot for a fucking berry.

"Of course. You know 'eius unicum filium'."

"No fucking way. How are you traveling?"

I looked at Blu. She shrugged, "My mom's been a travel agent for years.

"Don't go on the cruises, though, they suck."

"Bullshit."

"Ok, I'll tell you what. We'll tell you everything if you give us, say, five Mitchel Wagners."

He thought for a minute.

"One."

"Ok, how about four. Four Mitchel Wagners?"

The amazing orb scrunched up her face, "You know, Mitchel Wagner is a person, not a unit of currency."

"You sound like Davina."

"She's not wrong."

"Two. And that's all I can do." One of them actively cursed him out.

"Ok, I'm coming down."

I grabbed a joint and inhaled. One more hit, I kissed Blu on the lips. "You know, I really do adore you, chemotherapy bratz doll."

She smiled, "So don't get your ass killed, ok?"

I took another hit.

"Coming."

He stood there, flanked by Mitchel Wagner children. It wasn't not surreal. I held my hands up. My gun was in my pocket.

"So, I tell you how we can travel, and you give me two of these little shits here."

"Hey, fuck you, bitch." Said one of the Mitchels I didn't want.

"Not that one."

I opened my eyes wide to see the light in the room. I imagined Blu's smile and the way Albio tried to protect me and the way he talked to me like I was the most beautiful thing he'd ever seen. I imagined the taste of Los' lips and how strong he was protecting the bunny, and I realized I loved him, too. I was surrounded by people who had shown me in every way that they were love.

This guy was nothing. He was little. He hadn't even figured out who he was. I looked at him and the light shone all around him. He would be something once he let go and let the light in. He darkened and I could hear the Mitchels start to sing like a choir.

I saw her today at the reception

A glass of wine in her hand

I knew she would meet her connection

At her feet was her footloose man

The lights built into a giant swirls, wrapping the room up in congealed glow. The Mitchels were all dressed like choirboys, not a super-safe look in these Roman Catholic times.

No, you can't always get what you want

You can't always get what you want

You can't always get what you want

But if you try sometime you might find

There was a sign over their heads. It read "the Mitches." and it lit up, glowing with a shock of swirling light as they ended, harmonizing like a boy band.

You get what you need

I felt myself going. He wanted to know how we traveled.

"Like this."

I reached out to grab him where he stood, and I was suddenly behind him. I let out my breath and let the light wrap around me like smoke. I looked in front of me and saw myself.

Suddenly, I was back in the room. I was holding Ayjay from behind. I pulled my laser out and put it to his head.

The Mitchels started to scream.

Blu was next to me. She looked impressed.

She stepped over to the original strawberry and held her hand out. He handed her the gun.

He didn't want to watch me shoot his own head off from across the room.

"Ok, new deal. Information first. Why are you and EntheoGen doing this?

"Doing what?"

Blu hit him in the face. I wasn't expecting it, but I didn't hate it.

"You aren't a subtractionist?"

"Ha. One of you? No. You fuckers think that you can jump around fixing everything."

"So, you think we can't?"

The strawberry I was holding spoke up, "No one can. It's all fucked. All of reality is fucked. Even these kids know it."

Blu seemed pissed, "Because all you do is train them to be little monsters."

The tallest of the Mitchels spoke up, "Hey, bitch."

She continued, "See? The mouth on that kid. Fuck you, kid."

"It doesn't matter." Original Strawberry continued. "I've been all over time with that vest. It's all fucked. Nothing really matters. People die. People do the worst things imaginable to each other. It all needs to die."

The other Ayjay chimed in, "Yeah. It needs to all die."

"So, what does EntheoGen have to do with any of it?"

"Are you serious?"

"Yes. How bout some splaining."

"I'm Ayjay Marasco. This is EntheoGen. You really don't know?"

He continued, "Arnold James Marasco?"

"Oh my god. Up until this exact moment I thought it was Ayjay, like a name, not initials."

"That's not a name."

"Sure it is. I had an Indian friend named Ayjay."

"Do I look Indian?"

I looked at Blu. She looked at me and shrugged.

"Maybe. I don't know."

He seemed upset we didn't know. "Arnold Marasco? EntheoGen?"

"I think we're a no on that, still."

He was upset.

"That's about 200 times worse."

"Ouch."

I looked around. The alarms had stopped. That meant the chaos was winding down. We needed to get out of there. I started forward when the lights went out.

We were in a wide room with no windows. "Fuck," I thought, as I scrambled for the lights. Blu got there first.

Both versions of the Strawberry were gone. I looked over at the five Mitchels just standing there. The biggest one spoke.

"What the fuck are you looking at, bitch?"

Five minutes, and a gratuitous amount of the duct tape we had brought with us found us at room 117. I pulled off the lock Albio had placed and ushered our five Mitchels into a room filled with about ten more. All had their faces taped and hands tied.

I replaced the lock and grabbed Blu's hand. We walked down the hall into the bathroom. I dragged her into a stall and kissed her. She opened her mouth and let me suck on her tongue and I lost myself in her. We were still both feeling the effects of the drug and we let it wash over us. She pushed me against the door of the stall and sucked at me through my jeans, holding my ass in her hands. She pulled me closer and I could feel the want coming off of her like waves, crashing over each other, billowing like electric cycles, each projecting its own light. I could feel each wave hit, and hear the whir of it. She was pawing at me, desperate for how I tasted, and I remembered how she tasted, too and wished for a second, that everything tasted like that. The light swarmed around us, touching us. I looked down at the extra roll of toilet paper sitting on the ledge. It bent over and said, the hole working like a tiny mouth.

"It's a time wipe, baby."

The lighting had shifted. I kissed her and we made our way to the hallway. The lock was off the door to room 117 and it was empty. We moved to the side door and out.

The RV was parked right where it was before. We climbed into the deadening sound of fifteen Mitchel Wagners trying to get noticed. Each with duct tape around their heads.

Success.

I looked around.

Where was Albio?

KETAMINE RUSH

Chapter Eleven:

What to do on a Friday Night.

Alan placed the lock on the door.

In his head he heard the count from Sesame Street, "Ten. Ten Mitchel Wagners. Ha ha ha ha."

He shrugged. That was no more absurd than the rest of his day. The sprinklers had doused him completely as he had stopped to set the lock. He had heard somewhere once that you got wetter running in the rain than walking. This seemed like a bad time to try that out. He ran down the hallway looking for a room without a downpour.

There must be some room here no one cares enough about to prevent it from catching fire. He thought. That was the goal. About five doors later he found one.

This looked to be a locker room for the maintenance people. That was fantastic. He pulled the joints out of his pocket. They were a little wet, but not much. They would dry probably faster than he did.

There was a mirror over an old utility sink. This place seemed to really care about the workers, at no point did he think. He grabbed an old towel and began rubbing his hair. The towel had a familiar scent. Very homey.

It wasn't until he felt his hair dry did he recognize the smell of bleach on it. He rushed to the mirror.

Sure enough, it seemed like his hair was turning gold on top.

"Shit, Shit, " he rushed around. I put more water on his hair. It didn't seem to work. The process had already begun.

Now he had to walk around looking like a recent refugee from a boyband?

He sighed and started opening the lockers. None of them were locked, which made him question the whole idea of lockers at all, something he had never done before.

He found a shirt that fit and slid it over his head. Looking in the mirror, it seemed that his hair had definitely lightened on top a bit. He ran his hand through it. Still wet.

Sigh.

He sat and waited a bit. He was still trying to wrap his head around the fact that he had traveled into the past. Even if it was only a few hours, it was amazing. He leaned back in the overstuffed maintenance locker room couch and thought to himself.

I'm in the past.

It wasn't, like, the dinosaur past, but it was something.

He reached for the joints and grabbed two of them, knocking the other one over. It slid behind the couch. It looked unreachable. He tried to pull the couch out. It would take two of him to do that. For a minute, he toyed with the idea of going back a few minutes so there would be two of him. But he decided better. Best not to toy with the universe too much.

He took a deep breath and thought about Kerys. It's so strange how some people make you want to know them MORE, even when you know them quite a lot. He imagined what a picture of her from college might look like. He wished he could see her looking awkward. He was surrounded by people who seemed so at home in their own selves. Like they were never awkward. He lit the joint and inhaled. There was a familiar scent and taste. For the first time, he thought he could taste a tiny bit of orange. He stared at the row of lockers in front of him. The first one started to swing open, and a pile of oranges spilled out.

He laughed.

He laughed some more and inhaled again.

Light started to filter through the locker doors. The next door opened, and he could see branches, holding oranges, though the locker door. He remembered how his mom used to take orange slices and dip them in sugar on a plate for him as a treat after school. She would laugh about how it was bad for his teeth and too much sugar, but she knew he loved them.

And his teeth turned out fine.

For a second, Davi, Blu, and Kerys were kissing him, each in a row, each with their own unique kisses, each tasting slightly different, each with a light in them that was impossibly bright. His head fell to one side, and he suddenly knew that he belonged. How was he that lucky? He kissed Sean one of those nights.

He'd never had a lingering kiss like that with a man before. Where they just melted into each other without rushing or pushing for anything deeper. Playing with Sean was different than with anyone he'd ever been with. There was a kindness and an ease to him. He gave you the immediate feeling that no matter what you did, it was going to be ok. That YOU were ok. He was handsome and warm and strong in the way that makes people around him feel stronger than they thought they were.

And he'd had the chance to be really close to him. But not Los. Los was so quiet. He seemed like you'd need an invitation to step forward into his world. It looked like he was 4 for 5. He made a point to remedy that.

He laughed.

The light swirled and waved. The lockers opened in order, like dominoes dropping. A perfectly round beautiful orange fell out of it, onto the ground. The impact was booming and it echoed in Albio's head over and over. The orange split and a series of waves of light came pouring out of it. One after another. It built until the room was throbbing with light.

The light shifted from orange to yellow to white, and it pulsed and glowed, sending jello-like pieces of light spinning around his head. He looked into it and felt a recession, a darker area in the center. Suddenly, it was surrounded by sleekly cut orange slices, each delicately dipped in sugar, glistening, glowing.

And Alan wasn't alone anymore.

He was surrounded by people and the noise of laughter.

He looked up at a sign. He was standing in front of the Terminator Taters and Fries shop. A holographic sign in the window pulsed and rotated in 3-D. A robotic hand broke through the center of it and holographic glass went spinning everywhere while letters emerged.

It said, "You'll be back."

"Shit."

The Many Trials and Tribulations of Arnold Marasco.

Arnold Marasco came from a family of means.

But that didn't mean he didn't know how to work hard.

His father was in pharmaceuticals, so it seemed an easy way to enter the business world and make money. He started a company and bought a lab, even though he'd never stepped foot in one.

He was a businessman.

He hired the best people. The money people told him that he needed a great product. The research people told him that cancer was the most lucrative area of interest. The brand people told him that a cure would be well received immediately. The SEO people told him what to name it and how to talk about it. The PR people told him what color the package should be. And the thirty or so patents he had bought hoping that one would pay off showed him where to aim.

And that's how PROAXED™ came to market. PROAXED™ was the first product of its kind to cure cancer almost 60% of the time in lab animals and over 50% of the time in the first round of human subjects.

It was touted as a miracle.

And it was very expensive.

At this point, Arnold Marasco's company had invested millions in the drug. "The money people set the prices," Arnold told himself, "not me."

So, it wasn't his fault when people couldn't afford it.

It wasn't his fault that people were dying.

He was a businessman.

And it wasn't long before he was an even richer one.

Before LIFEMAX™ came out.

LIFEMAX™ cured cancer over 90% of the time. And for people who really needed it, it was free.

Suddenly the market for PROAXED™ crumbled. And Arnold Marasco was left with millions of cases and no buyers.

EntheoGen stock plummeted.

And Arnold Marasco was millions of dollars in debt.

So he started over. With AMPLICAZE™, a Diabetes control medication that had to be injected every month. Users of AMPLICAZE™ saw their insulin dependency drop dramatically. Arnold Marasco went to every investor he could to get the resources.

Real entrepreneurs don't use their own money.

And once again, the money people priced it.

It was, in a way, affordable. After all, how much would you pay to be insulin independent?

And people did pay. The business was back on top.

Until MERIZONE™ came out of left field. In 90% of cases, it completely eliminated the need for external insulin.

It essentially cured diabetes.

EntheoGen stock dropped dramatically again. And one more time, Arnold Marasco went out to investors with his hat in his hands.

EntheoGen's VARICON™ was 25% effective against IBS. And it dominated the Market.

Until GASTROMAX CS™ was released, effectively eliminating IBS almost completely.

EntheoGen's ECOLOX TABS™ helped some people manage their celiac disease well.

Until WEYVITALIN™ was released, pretty much curing celiac entirely.

Time and time again, Arnold Marasco found his stock falling as he woke up one morning to see some free or nearly free medication creating cures where his were only creating stopgaps. And his loyal customers?

Well, they defected.

Arnold Marasco stood on his balcony one night and wondered how it would feel when he hit the ground.

And after a lifetime of telling people to help themselves - to pull themselves up by their own bootstraps, he did it.

He helped himself.

The version of Arnold Marasco that appeared next to him on the balcony wore a futuristic looking vest and brought with him a younger man with blue skin. He had beaten the man nearly to death, and between the two of them, the Marascos were easily able to send him over the balcony instead.

And they traveled.

And they learned.

And Arnold Marasco, in all his variations, grew angry.

And they conspired with other Arnold Marascos.

Because sometimes they were the only ones he could trust.

He was an honest businessman. He followed the law, as much as it was possible.

How could he compete with a near infinite number of altruistic travelers virtue signaling their way through time, bringing what people may need?

For free?

What kind of a universe was it where an honest businessman couldn't survive?

That was the kind that needed to fucking die.

At that point, I sat in an RV chockful of Mitchel Wagner along with Davi.

"I think this is about ten more people than this thing can hold," Davina admitted. "On the plus side, though, it's kind of forcing out the piss smell."

She wasn't wrong. Too many people and not the one who should be here. "They have to find him."

Davi put her arms around me, "They will."

We stayed that way a minute.

She rocked me and said, in a baby voice. "We should take the tape off these people at some point. It's approaching a human rights violation."

I leaned into her hug, "I have no interest in anything they have to say."

"Yep. Me, neither. But let's do it." She handed me the scissors.

I turned to face the swirling Ocean of Mitch.

"Mitchels, I am going to start taking the tape off, so we can have a discussion."

They rustled around like a tiny herd of matching designer buffalo.

I stepped over to a larger one. This Mitchel was well fed. A fine cut of Mitchel, I thought.

I cut off the duct tape.

"Fuck you, ninja bitches. We're gonna kick your cunts off."

So, as you might imagine, that was a lot. First of all, no one said the word "ninja". I'm going to let you ruminate on what he actually said. But it was worse than the threat to kick our cunts off. Which, logistically, I wasn't sure how that would work. He clearly had no clue how a cunt worked or what would be needed to actually kick one off. And, at this rate, he would never learn. Which was, honestly, kind of a satisfying thought.

I put the tape back on and wrapped it tighter around his head. Nothing to see here, Mitch. Now, let's get those eyes covered, too, you fucking duct tape mummy.

"Ok, MItches. Notice that this Mitchel over here, let's call him 'Bitch Mitch,' gave up his right to ever talk or see ever again. And if you think it's going to feel good removing all that duct tape, think again, tiny Mitches. Consider that a cautionary tale. Now, who wants to have a conversation?"

A Mitch of about nine-years-old raised his hand. I figured, "How badly could this go?"

I carefully removed the tape. He had been crying.

"We want to go."

"You want to go home?" Davi asked.

He looked at his "brothers," and most of them shook their heads.

"No." He started crying.

I kneeled down, "Where is home?"

"In Peoria."

"And you don't want to go home?"

He shook his head vigorously.

"Do you want to go back to EntheoGen?"

They all shook their heads.

"No. They make us hurt things."

Davi looked resolute, "Where do you want to go?

Nine-year-old Mitchel Wagner looked at a room full of older versions of himself for some sort of guidance. But there was none. None of them could help. None of them knew anything but this.

None of them knew where they wanted to be.

None of them knew where they belonged.

Davi stood up. Suddenly I could feel what she was feeling. These were kids. These were kids being used to do something we didn't quite understand yet.

But how could Mitchel Wagner have grown up a good person like this? I may have said that out loud.

Davi leaned over to me and whispered.

"And why do you think they don't want to go home, either?"

Alan wandered around the convention.

First of all, the ATMs had no fees. This may have been one of the most remarkable parts of the entire trip. Alan swiped, wondering what this was going to look like on his bank ledger later. He thought he might have to be cautious as he was now officially unemployed.

He looked down at his four-hundred dollar balance. He took out two-hundred dollars.

His balance now read "$400 - reconciling."

He cocked his head.

He swiped again, taking out two hundred dollars.

The machine dispensed the money.

And his balance now read "$400 - reconciling."

It looked like maybe his bank had trouble connecting to eternity or the end of time or wherever the hell he was.

He swiped again, taking out four hundred dollars.

The machine dispensed the money.

And his balance now read "$400 - reconciling."

So, here is the thinking, when taking money out of an ATM that you know isn't yours, is what you're doing important? Do you need cash for it?

All good questions, Alan thought.

Thirty-two-hundred dollars later, there was a small line forming behind him. He looked back, shrugged, and moved on.

That was a unique experience. He was officially a bank robber. He stopped for a minute to look around.

Reconciling... .

Across the way was an open seat in front of the Time Cop Kettle Pop Corn Emporium. He tried saying that a few times to himself. He thought that naming these places might be the best job ever. A bag of popcorn later and he felt suspiciously better. And when the Capital One Police didn't appear, he felt even a little better than that.

This might be a good time to consider the situation.

Alan's situation in essence:

He had managed to time travel accurately once, about three hours into the past, with the help of partners. The second time, on his own, was effective, but not accurate. And he moved in space as well, Unless this was what the EntheoGen maintenance employee locker rooms looked like now.

After using one jay and dropping the other behind the couch, he was left with one, which meant that his next effort at traveling out of here had better be effective. This place seemed cool, but he didn't relish living the rest of his life here.

He wasn't 100% sure how this worked, but he thought there were things that he needed to do back in his own time. Would he be returned when he left? Or is all this taking up time he needed? There was no way for him to know.

Speaking of things to do, he was now surrounded by thousands of people who might have information they needed. Maybe that's why he ended up here. That felt teleological as hell, but he didn't know how this worked. Maybe you went where you needed to be.

There is no five. That's how bad this is. Oh, but he had a pocket full of cash.

He got a small Edge of Tomorroast Beef sandwich and a Back to the Fuchurro with cinnamon. And then he saw his first blue person.

As he soon discovered, there were a few timelines where the atmosphere of the Earth was decimated, leading scientists to have to genetically engineer their fellow humans to survive. In not an insignificant number of timelines, this turned the people a lovely and sort of elegant shade of blue.

There was a lot to look at.

He tried shooting water into Bill and Ted's little mouths as they lifted up off their little platforms into the timestream. Their tiny voices were the only things left.

"Be excellent unto each other."

The Looper Lobstercakes were better than the Sleeper Shrimp Rolls, which were, themselves, superior to the Time Bandits Burritos, which were, honestly, a bit bland.

He decided to walk it off a bit. It would be early evening soon.

It was really impossible to tell what time it was, but he had to admit the weather was brilliant. He wandered into the bathroom.

His hair was nearly blonde now at the tips. He ran some water through it again and tried to keep it from shooting out everywhere.

Not terrible, but not what he would have asked for at the barber shop. He pulled the remaining joint out of his pocket. It was still a bit wet to the touch. He had some time here before he could go.

Unless. Against the wall was a hand dryer. If he was careful, he could dry this thing and be ready to leave right away. He looked on the hand dryer trying to figure out how to turn it on the lowest setting. Oddly, the instructions were in both English and Dutch. He pressed a button.

And the joint flew out of his hand into the sink.

He jumped after it and tried to fish it out. His fingers nudged it as he reached and he watched as it cleanly slid down the drain.

He yelled out and reached his fingers into the drain. Suddenly he felt a tap on his shoulder. He looked to his right. A taller blue man with a mohawk pointed to a small sign flashing holographically in the mirror.

"Do not put fingers in the drain." Flashed.

"Steek geen vingers in de afvoer," immediately afterward.

"That's a weird fucking language," he thought.

"Yeah, man. Dutch is a funky thing," the man continued. "But these all have laser incinerators in them to handle garbage. Atomize your fingers in a second."

Alan looked down at the drain and his heart dropped from his chest.

"Thanks, man." Alan looked at the man. He really was a pretty shade of blue. He was wearing a shirt with a symbol in in - a nuclear symbol around a pentagram - with a line through it.

Alan pointed. "Fight the Nuclear Demon?"

The man looked down. "Oh, yeah. Big rally over by the Edge of Tomorrow. You going?"

Alan sighed. He wasn't going home anytime soon. At least he could learn something.

"That's the plan. I'm Al-Albio."

"Shuro Del. Nice to meet you."

Alan shook the blue hand trying not to look lost.

"Shuro. Hey. Want to walk over together?"

Alan's updated situation in essence:

All of the above still applied. But now, with the loss of the last joint, there was potentially no way to get back. He could steal a time vest, but did he know how to use one? Probably not. And he could end up in a Nazi concentration camp or inside a mammoth. Those were two uncomfortable places in world history. Let's not imagine any more.

He did still have a pocket full of cash. And, ostensibly, a bank account that giveth. He was surrounded by food, lodging, diversion, and more, as long as he could tolerate the occasional bad time travel film pun, and the one thing Alan had was a near endless tolerance for pop culture puns. The thought of which made him miss his job, from which he had doubtlessly been fired, for a moment.

He might be in a position to gather information. That worked. Information was something they needed.

He was hanging out with a Blue person. This was pretty cool. Almost all the people he know were some shade between pink and dark brown. He had come to think of them all as being "skin color." Shuro was more cerulean, which he now had to put into the category of "skin color," widening the tonal range of that category significantly.

There was still no 5, but man, he missed his friends. How did he get so attached to people in less than a week?

And how long would he be here?

It's not easy being blue. The actual color, not the person.

Shuro Kai had joined the subtractionists with his brother. Everybody knew it would happen one day. It was obvious.

You see, Shuro Kai was the living embodiment of question one.

Can you enjoy yourself anywhere? The Shuros did.

Earth in his timeline had experienced significant environmental upheaval. The genetic modification needed to survive until the planetary ecosystem could be repaired turned many people blue.

Shuro Kai was a seventh generation blue person. So was his brother Shuro Del. A lot of the blue people thought of themselves as particularly lucky. The eco-nightmare could have been a disaster. Instead, quick thinking by advanced people and scientists had turned it into a fun little artistic flair for humans.

And that's how everyone treated it.

Shuro Kai would often dress up as a clown or an alien from Star Trek, or some other cinematic creature, to travel to periods without blue people. This only seemed to amplify his joy at traveling. It was all a kind of cosplay to him. He was a time pirate. And that was his actual JOB.

How many people can say that they get paid, get bonuses, bet promotions, 401ks, etc. for doing what they love?

His first few years as a subtractionist were spent removing horror. The plans for a 100% effective water purification device invented by a young girl in Gambia in one time made a perfect gift for one of her ancestors three-hundred years earlier, trying to pull her people through a drought. Sure, it became a new timeline. But look at how people thrived in it.

It just worked.

A perfectly aged Malbec, from a vineyard that had perfected the grape made its way, under Shuro Kai's deft administration, to a middle east peace negotiation two-hundred years earlier, facilitating a deal that left everyone celebrating good feelings that were, admittedly, a bit amplified.

And a near universal cure for cancer made it to the Mayo Clinic, passing trials just in time for one of Shuro Kai's favorite musician's grandfather to reclaim his life and think about the future.

Maybe it was time to start a family, he thought.

Diabetes, irritable bowel syndrome, severe depression, He made them all his bitches.

And every time he returned, he walked under the sign over the door of the entryway that all subtractionists knew by heart. It was a mantra for every rat across timelines. And it always made him chuckle a little. Given his untimely end, there was a bit of sad irony in it. But that didn't stop the sign from being iconic.

It didn't stop it from being true.

And Shuro Kai would reach up and try to touch it whenever he got back, feeling the raised letters that read:

"Let no man be my enemy. But Fuck Cancer."

Chapter Twelve:

Yes, that cow.

The last thing in the world I wanted to do was to leave anybody alone with a room full of Mitchels, but this thinking about what Blu would do to them if they misbehaved was sort of the fucking wind beneath my wings, if you know what I'm saying.

"Try not to winnow the fold too much, ice cream scoop."

"Try not to Tuvix yourselves, Neelix."

I stopped for a second and looked at Davi. I think it was clear that I was Tuvok. I let it go, though, because I'm a reasonable bitch.

Davi and I went in the back. This place was truly disgusting. It held all the sadness of a Hoarders episode along with all the body fluids of a season of CSI Miami. I thought for a moment how satisfying it would be to blow this fucking thing up one day.

"Do you really think this is necessary?" I looked at Davi.

"Do you want to see what's really happening with these little monsters?"

I did, honestly, but I wasn't sure if I wanted to enough to jump around and make house calls on the Wagners.

"I met Janice, the mom. She seemed ok. Just a little Stepfordy."

Davi pulled her shirt off and handed me a joint. She pulled me onto the bed and kissed me.

"This part has nothing to do with traveling. I just like you."

That actually put me in the perfect headspace. I pulled her skirt up and realized that I was still wearing her panties. She felt warm and soft and wonderfully wet. I kind of wished it were all over me. I sank into the bed and kissed her hard. I wasn't used to kissing lips that were as full as mine and I liked it. She squirmed against me.

I held her arms over her head and grinded my leg into her. I whispered in her ear, "Get that all over me everywhere, please." And she started in earnest rubbing her pussy on me.

"I'm too fucking wet right now." She breathed at me. Her breath smelled like springtime when you woke up early and had nothing you needed to do, and you just wanted to feel the warm air on your stomach in bed all day from the open window.

"Oh, yeah? I need to see." She lit the joint and put it in my mouth so I could breath in. She took a hit as well as I moved downward and took her nipples in my mouth, one at a time. They were so full and hard and smooth. They felt, on my tongue, as though they were covered in a kind of micro velvet.

I took another hit and swirled my tongue on her bellybutton. I handed her back the joint and she breathed in the smoke, opening her legs so wide for me. I pushed her legs apart and up so I could wrap my whole mouth around her open pussy. It was slick and messy under my lips, and I thought about what a little bit of salt in liquid was for.

Electrolytes. The word popped into my head and I laughed.

I dug my tongue into her, trying to drink her up, licking the drops sliding down in between the cheeks of her ass. I could feel the joint starting to affect me, but it was nothing compared to how Davi affected me.

She shook and made noises like an animal and my head tried to translate this beautiful, dignified spiritual girl turning into a raw, physical creature under my mouth. She must have read my mind, pulling at my head and forcing my face deeper into her. I loved watching polite, demure Davina change into this. I sucked on her harder. She moaned and started the chant, "Don't stop. Don't stop."

There was a rhythm to her words, a kind of metronome-like bounce that my heart started to sync to. My tongue shifted to her rhythm. I opened my eyes wide and saw her lithe belly rising up over a puff of dark curly hair, rising and falling in the same rhythm. The light glinted off the sleek dew of her hair, as tiny beads of sweat slid down, bouncing in order, in rhythm.

I wanted that sweat in my mouth, along with all of her. The idea that Davina could be too wet was laughable. I wanted her as a hurricane, a fucking river. The light flowed over her belly now, wrapping around the tiny bubbles, swirling in time. And it rose up with each "Don't stop," falling and congealing around us, painting us into the bed in liquid light. I opened my mouth for her and opened myself up to everything.

Her rhythm continued without change into the two most magnificent words in the world while I tried to catch all of her in my mouth. The light spun us and parted, leaving a perfect space for us, just the right size for us.

And I felt the air change. I didn't want to lift my head from her. She tapped me on the shoulder. I looked around.

We were in a room, walls covered in faux wood and stone, black and gray carpet on the floor.

It worked.

I kneeled up and kissed her on the lips. I was still there between her legs. She was sitting, holding herself up with her arms behind her. She was smiling the way that makes you want to do anything for her.

I was totally still high.

"I just realized how much I love those two words."

She laughed, "Oh, you mean 'I'm cumming?'"

"Those are the ones. Maybe it's the delivery."

"Oh, yeah. We should experiment and see."

Suddenly a voice boomed behind us.

"Can I grab that carpet first?"

Davi jumped up to get her top on.

"Oh. Paul, is it? Janice needs these dimensions again. I think she's just gonna replace the carpet entirely. It's nothing you guys did. She just has new color ideas. It sucks, but we all want the Wagner place looking good."

Paul looked at me. If I had pulled this off, he would just respond without looking down at his nametag and embroidered "Jiffy Carpet Cleaners" shirt. I prepared myself to fight or run if he did.

"Well, no skin off my teeth. It's twelve by ten exactly. I got about five other places I got to be. You can handle this? Do you need me to write that down?"

"Nope. Twelve by ten."

He shifted his look over to Davi, raising his eyebrows.

Davi looked at me impressed, then him, "Yeah, I'm feeling better. Just a little... My time, you know."

Now, I was impressed. Most men know so little about menstruation and are so unwilling to discuss it that it makes a perfect out for almost anything. Not feeling good? Period. Passed out topless on the floor? Period. Accidentally kill a man with an icepick? Period.

That last one would be nice sometimes. I wanted to try it.

Paul started walking out. Turning to us, "You got keys?"

I waved him on, "Yeah, we'll lock up, no worries. I know Janice probably gave you that lecture at least twice."

He snorted, "Yup. Have a good one, ladies."

We watched him walk out. Davi slapped my arm.

"That was fucking amazing. You have to teach me what you just did."

"What can i say? I got that 26th century mojo."

"My phone isn't connecting."

"Sure it is. It's just not connected here. Your other phone is probably closer to a tower. You sort of 'cloned' your sim. But they both have the same ICCID, so only one can access the network."

A note for the reader:

> So, for anyone reading this, yes, that is true in theory, but in reality, maybe not. I put this in here to be responsible. We're telling a story glamorizing sex, drugs, rock and roll, bisexuality, polyamory, and more things that, if you have to be honest with yourself, you've watched at least one video of on youporn and done stuff to yourself. Do I also want to glamorize cell phone sim card fraud? I have to draw the line somewhere and honestly, you're welcome, T-mobile, this is where I do it. I still think it's possible all phone carriers suck, but I'm also not looking to sit in a wooden box during a class action lawsuit for promoting fraud.
>
> Continuing.

She looked around, taking it all in.

"Where are the Wagners, anyway?"

I grabbed the remote of the lip of the table in front of us and clicked the television on. I loved visiting everything after the 20th century where every single piece of technology seemed to want to scream the date and time at you like you were an ex-boxer sliding into that deep neurologically damaged dementia that makes you want to touch everything around you first to see if it isn't cake. Try figuring out what day it was in Chaucer's pre-sewer system England when half the people can't read and most have no jobs and few understand what the calendar actually is or why they need to know the time at all. Also, no sewers. Life gets way sexier the more you hide away human waste.

Hide that shit.

In the corner of the television screen, on the menu, the date and time.

"If I had to say, I would bet that they're picking up a bunch of boy scouts to bring them back before they go camping."

"It's Tuesday."

"We'll be here soon. So let's figure out what we need to and get out."

"Fair. Although I feel like it's been Tuesday a lot."

Davi and I tried to do a complicated handshake. It really wasn't terrible. I tried to put it out of my mind that I didn't know where Albio was.

"And we need to not change too much. We don't want to make a branch."

"We are ghosts. Got it."

"We are smoke."

"We are Seal Team 7, hiding in a bayou."

"We are shadows, slipping through keyholes."

We slinked upstairs. Two bedrooms and a bathroom. I went into the parents room, Davi slipped into Mitchel's like one of those shadows we discussed.

The parent's room was as you might expect. Possibly a little messier than most. Nothing to talk about, really. Davi called out to me and I moved to Mitchel's room.

"What do you think?"

"Hm," I looked around. "In your life, have you ever seen a kids' room cleaner than the parents?"

"Yeah, Mitchel doesn't live in this room."

"How can you tell?"

She pulled back the comforter. There was no fitted sheet. She moved to the dresser.

Empty. No dirty magazines. No socks. Nothing.

"That is suspect, for sure. Or 'sus' as the kids say, now."

"You are so hip."

She looked around, "So, where does he live here?"

We moved back downstairs and took another look. I checked out the kitchen and again, Davi caught it. She met me at the counter with a framed picture.

"So, what do you see here?"

Young, fourteen-year-old Mitchel looked normal, flanked by Janice and Glen, his parents. Something felt wrong to me. And then I saw it.

"Fuck."

"Yep. Mitchel has blue eyes. He's fourteen, so they are the color they're going to be. His parents? Brown."

"They aren't his parents."

"Not genetically.

"So, who are they? Is Mitchel Wagner adopted?"

"Not according to the history I know." I stared at his face. It looked normal. "Is that all there is here?"

Davi pointed to a door, "Basement."

We made our way down the stairs and were instantly hit by the smell.

It smelled like death.

There was a washing machine, a dryer, a sink. The basement was tiny, far smaller than it should have been.

I walked over to the far wall and felt. There was a slit in the wall, about four feet from the left side. I pushed inward and it clicked, snapping back.

This wasn't high security. No one was hiding anything.

They were in the middle of Peoria.

They thought no one would ever come looking.

Behind the wall was an abattoir. It was horrible. It looked nearly identical to the classrooms at EntheoGen. The new corpses of animals were all over. Charts on the wall showed how to accomplish a dissection, how to kill someone. There were belts and torture equipment hanging from the wall and a cot in the corner.

This is where Mitchel Wagner lived.

This is where Janice and Glen were working to raise him to be a sociopath.

They took a little boy and did all this to make him into a monster. Davi ripped off a poster extolling the virtues of rape. And as she did, she saw the symbol behind it.

We both saw it.

The front door upstairs slammed shut.

The Wagners were home.

I pulled the joint out and lit it. I handed it to Davi and she inhaled. As I turned to find a place to stand near her, I bumped into the biggest corpse in the room.

There was, on a table, a cow that had been tortured horribly, its face removed. It seemed by the grotesque arrangement of its mouth it had been alive throughout the process. How could any child be raised in this and not become evil?

I started to feel sorry for the Mitchel Wagners of the universe. Someone had decided that he would be evil and they made it true.

They chose it, not him.

Davi passed the joint back to me and I sucked it in. I was still a little high and I hoped it was enough. I looked over at Davi. How could this girl be this quick? I grew up to be this, five-hundred years into a future that prepared me for it. Not her.

She was just this.

She was scary smart. Suddenly I really saw her. Her face was like a universe all by itself with tiny freckled stars set all over, each one full of life and power and brilliance. I kissed her and the smell of the room washed away. I put my hands on her waist and I felt energy pass from her skin to my fingertips filling me with power and life. I leaned in closer to focus on a single freckle and I saw it morph and change into a tiny solar system with a beautiful orange sun lit and alive like it had billions of years to go.

I heard the rhythm of her breath as it picked up. The closer I got to her, the faster she breathed, the more it built. I realized that mine rose when I touched her, too, and we matched now, in harmony, aligned. The horrors of this room disappeared as the light flowed from her tiny sun and enveloped us. It built into a ring with a beautiful, brilliant hole in it, and I was able to see it as a doorway for the first time.

I put my hands on her ass and kicked the table, sending the contents into the hole, the dissected cow. It spun one direction until it got smaller and disappeared. Davi laughed and spun around, her hands all over me. I finally realized what we needed to travel as the light thumped and throbbed and her laughter built, making me want to fall away into it.

And then it was dark.

We were on the bed in the back of the RV.

And I think I understood how to travel now.

On the way to the rally, Alan had the chance to learn about a hero.

Or, at least that's how Shuro Del talked about his brother. His face lit up when he talked. Shuro Del was taller than Alan by at least six inches, which made him one of the tallest people he'd ever seen. His skin seemed smoother than was humanly possible, which might have been an artifact of him being the most fascinating hue of cerulean blue. He wore black pants and just his vest, exposing a barrel chest underneath, blue and smooth.

To Alan, he looked like a superhero himself. Shuro Del continued.

"He was my younger brother. The last time I saw him, though, he might have been a little older."

"That must have been confusing."

"Just sort of par for the course, right? It's expected." He laughed.

Alan considered that. It wasn't the weirdest thing he had been forced to consider in the last few days.

"He worked a lot, huh?"

"Oh, Jellica..."

Alan had heard him say that about four times now. It must have been some sort of future god or even just a future expression. Shuro launched into a detailed timeline of his brother helping people. IBS, Hunger, Cancer, Diabetes, etc. No horror was too big or too small for Shuro Kai.

"Every day. He wanted to do good, you know. He used to tell me when we were kids he was going to put on a vest and no one would ever go hungry again."

"Damn. That's a big ambition."

"That was Kai. That was us, really. You see this?" Shuro opened his vest and showed Alan a symbol on the inside, it was a symbol of a hand with a sun in it.

"Kai had this too. All the Shuros do. It means that we want to bring light to the world with everything we do with our hands. To carry light"

Kai seemed like good people

"And I know this thing did something to him."

Shuro Del pointed up at a thirty foot holographic demon with a symbol burned into its chest. It was the EntheoGen symbol.

Alan looked around.

They had arrived at the Rally.

He listened to the speakers. There were just twenty or thirty people. They were all mostly disheveled anxious people.

They called themselves rats. They talked about how this thing they knew nothing about ended everything in every timeline and none of them could get there. Each got up and told their story about how they had lost a partner, a friend, a brother to the end of time timeline. About how they went and never came back.

About how all that was left was this symbol.

The EntheoGen symbol.

A dark skinned woman with a mass of dark curls got up to speak. Her name was Reina. She seemed to know more than almost anyone about the catastrophe at the end of time. But still now what Alan knew.

Alan leaned over to Shurro. "You guys know what that symbol is, don't you?

"It's the Nuclear Demon at the end of time."

Alan stopped.

They didn't know about EntheoGen.

"Hey, man. After this, do a bunch of you all want to sit down, get a drink, and share information?"

He showed him his bulging wallet.

"I'm buying."

Sean and Los sat on the steps outside the massive entryway to EntheoGen pretending to play rock, paper, scissors. Albio still hadn't appeared and they were starting to get worried. He was either trapped in this building or trapped in the time stream trying to get back.

Neither one was a great option.

And while tracking him down in the timestream seemed difficult, the other one was doable.

I mean, how big WAS this building anyway?

So they waited.

About an hour after the RV drove off, opportunity drove up in the form of two maintenance people roughly the same size as the two of them. They got out of their vehicle and started around to the back of the building.

The area in back of the building was crawling with people, so this had to be done before they got back there. Luckily, the two stopped to grab a hot dog from the vendor in front. Sean and Los looked at each other. Workers stalling before work? Definitely the kind of people they needed. They walked up to them and made a motion to pay for the hot dogs.

Your money's no good here, they seemed to say.

The two workers smiled. Maybe hotdogs each?

Sean clapped the bigger one on the back.

Not a problem.

They took their dogs and sat down, all four of them.

Los opened his shirt and showed them the bag of weed.

Maybe today wouldn't be a work day, after all.

Alan sat in a chair at the Interstellar Wine Cellar with Reina and Shuro and thought about how to approach this. He decided, in the end, to just come clean.

"I'm not a time traveler."

"Well, you are at least a little." Reina noted.

Shuro added. "You're here."

"I am. Ok, let me try again. I'm not a subtractionist. I'm very on board with what you guys do. Two of my friends are. They're back in the 21 st century right now. They went back trying to figure out the Mitchel Wagner issue."

"Which, in our time, has been solved." Reina jumped in, taking a swig of her Peggy Sue got Margarita.

Shuro Del affirmed that. "My timeline, too. Nearly all the timelines had Mitchel Wagner taken out of the picture."

Alan continued, "So, I don't know what that means and I probably don't want to know, but my friends come from a little earlier than you. They showed up in my timeline and their vests stopped working. Do you know what could cause that?"

"Yes, but how do we know that you won't do something stupid with it?" Asked Shuro, calling for another Army of Darkness Berry Daiquiri. They actually looked pretty good, Alan thought as he called for one, too.

"What if I tell you what that symbol means?" Alan pointed to Shuro's shirt.

"The Nuclear Demon?"

"Yes, but over five-hundred years before that, in my timeline, it's the logo of a company called EntheoGen."

"Wait, a company logo?"

"What company is it?"

"In my timeline, they're a giant pharmaceutical company. Run by someone named Arnold J. Marasco."

"Why is a pharmaceutical company trying to end the universe?"

"And how?"

Alan asked, "How does it end? What happens?"

Reina breathed out, "We don't really know. All we know is that we can't access the area. No one can get in or out for about thirty years before the event. And then it just ends. There isn't anything after it."

"My brother sent the message. With the symbol. And then disappeared."

Alan thought, "Was he going forward? Did he know?"

"As far as I knew, no. He didn't. He was heading back in time to do his job."

"What exactly was he doing?"

Shuro pulled a wig and nose out from his bag. "We blue people travel as clowns very often when we go to the pre-blue past."

Reina smiled and winked at Shuro, "We call it the drab past."

"He went back to the 21 st century to bring a diabetes cure."

"And then, for some reason, went forward and then disappeared?"

"Yes. And your friends are in that time, you say?"

"Yes. It's where I come from."

"So, you're not wearing a vest. How did you get here?"

Alan leaned back into his chair. "This is going to require another round."

Sean and Los wandered through the halls of Entheogen. It was not yet time to panic, so they weren't. It seemed like the people they saw were all trying to clear away the chaos caused by the explosions.

Los pumped his chest out a little at that idea.

When they were here before, they had gone to the topmost floor. Of the two open doors, they chose one. That's how they got these badges and the coherent light guns.

There was no reason they couldn't go back to the other door, right? For all they knew Albio might be there.

Using the badges, they took an elevator to the seventh floor and stepped out into the hallway. A maintenance person was still trying to mop up. They nodded at him and he nodded back. In his mind, Sean said, "Fuck management."

The man looked up and stopped mopping for a minute. In his mind, he said, "yeah, fuck management."

Sean raised his fist in the air. He may have still been a little high.

They moved into the room they had missed last time.

On the table in front of them was even more swag stolen from time travelers - subtractionists who had been to this time.

Guns, equipment, even vests. Scattered all over the table.

Some were being taken apart, clearly to see why they had stopped working.

Sean found a bag in the corner. He looked over at Los.

And there was a knock at the door.

Los shrugged and walked calmly over to the door. It was important to act like they belonged there. He was ready for what was on the other side.

He thought.

A blonde Albio stepped in the room and closed the door.

"Hey, guys, got to go."

Sean and Los exchanged glances and shrugged.

Mission accomplished. They all left.

Albio ran back in and grabbed some things and threw them in the bag.

He looked back.

Now, mission accomplished.

Chapter Thirteen:

I named all my Stuffed Animals after you.

Back in the RV, I looked away for a second and Bitch Mitch made a break for it. He slammed his head into my stomach and threw himself at the door. We'd moved the RV right by a park with fewer people around and he took the opportunity to barrel across the cement entryway. I jumped out after him.

Blu had been guarding the door and she was taken by surprise. She was a little faster than I was. We ran across the park as he did a circuit of the jungle gym. I want to remind you that he was still wrapped up like a duct tape mummy. The fact that he couldn't see or likely hear made it no easier to recapture him.

Blu cut him off on one side and I trapped him on the other. He did a flip and ran the other way, using the force or some shit. I honestly did not know.

I looked at her. Someone taught Mitchel Wagner Jedi Parkour? That sucked.

He dove through the swings and the lollipop followed. I got momentarily tangled in the chains and fell over. And I could see.

Blu jumped after him and bounded down the street, Jedi Bitch Mitch about twenty-five feet ahead of her. I struggled to keep up. I started to wish that Sean and Los hadn't stayed to wait for Albio.

What were we thinking that the three of us could handle fifteen identical juvenile delinquents? How did Blu do this alone?

He was approaching the opening to the street. Once out there, people would see and it would be hard to recapture the little bitch. Or he would be turned into greasy smudge Mitch by an errant Amazon Prime delivery truck. Both sketchy outcomes. I grit my teeth and pushed myself.

One last sprint.

And then, suddenly, Bitch Mitch's body went flying to my right as though hit by an invisible boxing glove.

Blu and I banked and ran to the body. He was unconscious but alive. It was almost like there was a leash on him that was pulled taught. I heard Blu yell out and saw her jump from the corner of my eye. She ran to throw her arms around him. Walking alongside Sean and Los was a blonde version of Albio, exactly as I had first met him at the convention.

I breathed in what felt like the first time in a day. I wrapped myself around him and Blu.

"Were you where I think you were?"

"I was. And I think I know what's going on."

We dragged Bitch Mitch back to the RV, locking the Mitches in there securely. This gave us the chance to talk for a minute.

I sat in the center swing and pulled Albio next to me. "So let's see it."

He retrieved the concussion gun and held it out.

"So, you're just a gun collector now? Just guns everywhere?"

"Only used twice." He winked at me.

"So, what did you learn, cowboy?"

"A lot. First of all, most of the people I met were on the job dealing with these guys- Mitch Wagner. "

"That tracks. It's been a giant issue."

"So, what happens if everybody is off trying to stop this guy? What does that look like?"

"Well, people aren't doing a lot of other things. Helping people out, etc."

"It means a lot of dead Mitchel Wagners." Blu speculated.

"So, you guys, the subtractionists, you would kill him?"

I sighed, "We don't want to, necessarily. But the alternative is a war that makes World War 2 look like a game of Battleship in a fucking bathtub."

"And it's because he's so awful?"

"Hey, go see for yourself. He's a fucking monster already."

Albio looked at Davina. She shrugged, "I'm not disagreeing. I kind of want him dead myself."

"And... The result is a whole series of timelines where Mitchel Wagner is dead. In very similar ways."

"In nearly identical ways."

"And those timelines are so similar, they might merge?"

Los looked up, "They're TRYING to create a confluence?"

Blu looked confused, "Why?"

"That's what I was trying to figure out. The third coolest thing I learned, actually. The energy in a confluence that size is unstoppable. If every timeline looks basically the same and they start to merge like tributaries, the remaining current is too strong. "

Los chimed in, "It jumps the bank."

"It washes away the edges and expands."

"And no one can get in. no one can stop it."

"This is just a metaphor," I jumped in.

Albio continued, "But it's real. If Mitchel Wagner were a good leader or a mediocre leader or even a good regular person, he might do something worthwhile, a hundred different diverse ways."

"But dead Mitchel is dead Mitchel."

"Exactly."

"So, why did you take my battery and send me here, Gunsmoke?"

"That is the second coolest thing I learned."

Suddenly the RV started up and moved forward. It did a quick doughnut and came right at us.

We jumped up and dispersed as it rammed the swing set. One of the Mitches must have gotten loose and hotwired it, leading me to think that maybe their criminal training had advanced further than I'd thought.

The RV ran over the flowerbed, across the central gazebo in the park, smacked into the spring horses, and shook it all off, taking off toward the busy intersection that Bitch Mitch had been trying to reach. The RV seemed to vibrate just as aggressively when seen from the outside as it did from within.

We yelled after it.

That didn't seem to do much, but it felt a little satisfying.

Little fuckers.

I looked back at the guys. Blu looked down and sighed.

Albio grabbed my arm and kissed me.

"You know where to meet me. At the Edge. Bring this."

He handed me the bag.

And disappeared into a swirl of open light.

I stared at the space he was standing in just one second earlier and paused.

"That's probably the third thing he was about to get to."

Alan, Shuro Del, and Reina were about as drunk as they could get, but they had a kind of plan, the very first part of it was to get some coffee and see if the plan made sense when sober.

A lot of the plan depended on things beyond their control.

But Alan had faith. And that was a remarkable thing to him. Sometimes you can know someone for just a few days and just believe in them.

Like he believed in her.

In the end, it's hard to tell, when grounded, how long you've been there. The Buddha said that it took ten-thousand years to achieve enlightenment. Sean would counter that with the fact that Buddhism really says it takes ten-thousand things.

Ten-thousand things you have to notice and see.

Ten-thousand things that swim around all of us that we miss.

And, honestly, Alan would tell you, it's the first few thousand things to see that are the hardest.

Once you start to see, You realize that the visible universe outpaces the invisible one. you start to realize that the universe itself isn't sentient, but it has its own will. It has directives. It has methods and even, in some way, plans.

So, it could have been ten-thousand years.

but Alan thought it was more like a year-and-a-half.

And throughout that time, he'd seen her there. He'd even seen different versions of her.

But he never approached her. It wasn't time yet.

He'd worked and planned.

And Shuro Del and Reina stayed and worked with him.

And waited.

Reina placed it on the table between them. It was only a few inches around.

Red. Rubber.

Alan asked first. "So, how does it work?"

Reina explained as though it were her baby. Which it was.

"You press the front, here, and it blocks the beacon across the entire timeline."

"Everywhere?"

"Yes."

"So, we get this back to the 21 st century and all the vests will stop working?"

"Every one."

"No more adding to the confluence?"

"We need to get these back to other timelines when people snap back."

Shuro looked nervous, "We're about to kill every vest. And we haven't made as much headway into traveling without them."

Alan was hopeful. "We will. You have to trust me."

Someone with a little less faith would have lost hope already.

He picked up the red rubber ball.

So, I know what happened from here, if you don't mind me taking over.

I slid in next to him and whispered,

"So, that's how you did it?"

And he turned.

And I kissed him as hard as I could.

Which, it turns out, is pretty fucking hard. And toothy.

I handed him the bag, t-shirt, concussion gun, a couple of pieces of paper.

"You should be sad you missed the fucking orgy it took to get me here."

He burrowed his head into my neck.

I felt like we had a lot to figure out.

"Didn't you have an RV full of Mitchel Wagners?"

I shook hands with his friends. The blue one's name was Shuro. The woman's name was Reina.

"I did. And they are in the right place right now. I sort of sidebarred that discussion. But our big issue right now is that we need to figure out how to travel without drugs, without other people, without vests…"

Reina jumped in, "And without a beacon."

"Right." I looked at the rubber ball. It was so tiny.

"I think I can help with that."

They stared at me.

"Back home, one of our friends, Sean, he kept talking about religion, about prayer. And we shushed him. Over and over. Maybe too much."

Reina asked, "I don't understand. There is a religious component?"

"Not really, but religion is a sort of guide. What we discovered from the drugs is that the light that swirls spacetime is endemic to the universe. It doesn't need to be created, just recognized. "

"The same kind of lights that the vests use?"

"Not exactly, but close. What if the universe is not sentient, but is willful?"

"Those aren't the same things?" Shuro looked confused.

"Religion tells us to adore god - to love him. A peacock isn't sentient, but it has the will to be proud. And to recognize it when something is looking. The universe can perceive our awe."

"I'm not sure about that." Reina prodded.

"I'm learning to look. When I look at Albio here, I see a light. And the universe knows that he is something special. Imagine it points its finger here in pride. This is a beautiful thing. And that place where the finger touches reality becomes slightly more transparent."

"It lets light through."

The light surrounds him, but it's endemic to the universe. The drugs help us really see each other. They open us up to awe, to gratitude. To want. They expose our desire to connect to a beautiful moment or an important moment or someplace we need to be. And we see it."

Albio was understanding, "And we step though."

"I was starting to understand. And then what cemented it was your face, when you dropped these off." I showed him the bag.

Albio looked over at Shuro and Reina, "Ok, I haven't done that, yet. Can I still do it?"

Reina put her hand on Albio's, "Yeah, there's time. We're coming from a grounded place. We slide back into the timeline."

Shuro glanced at me. "That reminds me. We need to go over our part of the plan."

We spent about a day going over what Shuro, Reina, and I would do once Albio hooked up with me.

And then we practiced traveling for a few weeks.

I admit that The first time that Albio and I made it work without the drug, he may have been inside me. We needed to get to a place where sex wasn't needed either, but it seemed like once you let yourself fall into someone like that, to really see how big they were in the light of the universe, it was hard not to...

Well, jump them.

Finally, we were able to move from one place to the other in the convention space unaided. In a way, it wasn't hard in that space. There was so much to look at, so much pure beauty. So much that the universe might be proudly pointing at, jumping up and down, flashing lights for us to see, to take in, to be aware of.

It was a place where the very space around us wanted us to move through it.

I dragged Albio to the Judgment Day Juice bar pointing out the opening of the cave-like area where we had met. I handed him a concussion gun and the t-shirt and a note.

"I feel like it's your first day of school."

"Well, now you killed it."

"Behave, Alan. Listen to the teacher."

He laughed. "I'm Albio now, I think."

I adjusted his shirt. I noticed a fountain a few feet away. I wet my hand and ran it through his hair. "Ok, Albio. Go get her."

He started forward. Then turned to me.

"I'm going to say this to you, not to her. And then I'm going to walk away."

He was the most transparent person I'd ever met. I kissed him.

He whispered it and then disappeared.

I watched her see him for the first time.

She would love him too, eventually.

And I went on to finish the plan.

"So we're just going to steal it?" I asked Reina. I was starting to like her easy, no nonsense way.

"Yes. In a way, we already stole it," she smiled.

"That's the only kind of time heist I like. The kind where we already did it."

Shuro equivocated, "Or failed."

"What's up with the blues over here?"

"Well, there is a timeline where this didn't work. And one where it did."

"One?"

"At least one. We know of."

"We need to do this to avoid the confluence, right?"

"Exactly. We need diversity in the timelines.

"So, maybe it's good if we don't succeed in every timeline."

Shuro looked relieved, "That's actually not a bad point."

"Unless we die. Because that would be objectively bad for us."

"I can deny none of that."

I did like her.

Let's go back in time a little.

In 1993, this amazing filmmaker named Harold Ramis made one of the most enduring films of all time.

It was called Groundhog day and it starred a famous and beloved comedian and a beautiful quirky and funny leading lady.

In the movie, a television reporter became cynical, overly self-engaged, even angry at the world. On a visit to a small town, an invisible force, never explained in the film, created a dilemma for him that became known as the groundhog day time travel trope.

Every morning, he woke up to the the same song at the same time on the same radio station. Walking through his day, he eventually realized that he was living the same day over and over. In a kind of surly way.

He became despondent and tried to kill himself. Each time, he ended up back in bed, with that same song going on. He tried to get rich, to get laid, to get everything he wanted, but he just ended up miserable again, and trapped in the inscrutable time loop.

Eventually, he managed to escape the same day over and over again. Harold Ramis' original script said it was after that ten-thousand years we talked about. When you break it down realistically, he was probably in the loop for about thirty-five years.

Still a significant amount of time. Finally, he discovered that engaging in truly selfless acts, without expectation of personal enrichment was what was needed to end the time loop.

In his newfound enlightenment, he actually did manage to get the girl.

She eventually left him the next year for another guy in Four Weddings and a Funeral.

You see, what I did there was to pretend the movie was real.

And so was the next one. And Andie McDowall was the same character.

It's fun and silly, and this is the kind of things that happens to movies sometimes a few hundred years after they get put out.

Someone bootlegs it and writes a new copy on the box. Someone else edits versions of it together with some other movie, etc. This is how the original Star Wars trilogy eventually became a rom com.

Because video editing tools are so freely available that maybe it's a good plan not to trust anything.

At any rate, the movie had gone through a lot of permutations, even becoming an animated kids cartoon in 2230. The original had been copied, edited, merged with other films, etc. for years.

In the 24th century, scientists got a copy of the movie and thought, this is a great idea. They worked together and, about a billion dollars later, had invented a time ground. This did essentially what was being done in Groundhog Day. They sold it to the biggest entertainment company in the world that used it to start a, you guessed it…

Time traveler convention.

Everyone was invited. And another billion dollars later, the snapback technology was developed, letting people return to where they came from.

The convention is massive and sprawling. It gets bigger all the time. And it never stops making money, incrementally. Every day, it makes more. And if you do the math, you may see how that works as the number of people there rise exponentially.

In homage to the origins of the ground, the scientists who built it originally built the ground into the image of the man who inspired it. It was shaped to resemble the comedian who shaped that role and really made it come alive.

Unfortunately, hundreds of years, bootlegs, re-edits, cartoons, and more led to an image that didn't really resemble the comedian very closely. And this disparity in image wasn't helped by the sign at the base of it, honoring him.

A sign that said, simply, "Bill Murphy- Groundhog Man."

To further add to the generalized aura of misunderstanding surrounding this piece of science/art, you might notice two large buck teeth clearly visible on the "Groundhog Man."

It was a silly statue. A massive failure in an artistic sense.

But, scientifically, a one-of a kind, billion dollar item.

And Reina and I?

We were going to steal it.

When he was finally ready, Alan waited by the Judgment Day Juice Bar. He had seen her there over and over.

Kerys.

He had thought about this moment for so long.

This is before they met.

This is earlier Kerys.

And he was ready for this. He knew enough about what needed to happen. He wanted to actually meet her for the first time when he was at his best. Not stripped and tied up in the back of a pizza van or wandering lost around this convention with no way back.

He tried to consider everything he knew about time travel. If he did this wrong, he would overwrite what had happened between them? He didn't want to do that. And was he here already?

No idea.

But.

It was easy for him to forget how beautiful she was when he was there, looking at her every day, waking up with her. But here, seeing her at a distance, by herself, before they had met.

It was impossible not to realize. He pulled out the note that his Kerys had given him. Iit read, simply...

"You are worm poop."

He shrugged, sliding the gun and t-shirt into his bag.

About thirty yards ahead of him, she turned and started walking.

He looked around and saw the cave. A large sign over it said, "Ancient Artifacts of Time Travel." It looked dark and out of the way.

And actually sounded kind of interesting, anyway. He hoped this was the right place. The cave.

He slid in and tried to lose himself in the shadows, watching her.

It suggested that time travelers had been to Earth before. Maybe a lot. He was never really much of a conspiracy theorist or anything like that. He had just assumed that Egyptians built the Egyptian stuff and Greeks built the Greek stuff.

That seemed reasonable to him.

But now that he knew time travel was real, what if they were involved in history in ways he never knew. What if everything he really thought he knew about history was a lie.

He kept on learning. More every day.

The hall was huge. It took a second for his eyes to adjust. At first glance it seemed like he must have been in the giant worm section. Nearly every display had a giant puffy worm in it, sometimes exploding into a wash of blood, sometimes eating an unwitting time traveler. He leaned in closer to look.

But, seriously, what the fuck was with all these worms?

"Boo!"

He jumped and fell on his ass.

"And that's how you get eaten by a Giant Blood Worm, bitch. Boom."

He looked up. Kerys reached down to help him up.

"I'm sorry, man. That was too good."

He tried not to stare, "I should stay down here."

He thought back to the note.

"I'm just worm poop now."

"Oh, we're role playing now. Nice. I'm Cleopatra."

"Cleo. You know I was just trying to save you from the worm."

"And what makes you think I need saving, Timberlake?"

"Oh, you don't. You could kick that worm's ass. I just need to save someone today or they take away my superhero license."

"Well. You could save me from the deadly ablation of starvation, pretty boy."

She thought he was pretty. "Damn. That sounds urgent. Where should I carry you, in case you pass out?"

"Do you know what the fuck a French Mexican taco is? I'm curious."

She tousled his hair. "Also your hair is wet, Captain Justice. Is it raining?"

"Fighting injustice is a messy business. Rainy."

"If you can't afford an umbrella, can you swing a taco?"

"Hey, I have a million umbrellas. I'm basically made of umbrellas. You don't love prancing in the rain?"

"I don't prance, Umbrellicus Rex."

"You're missing out. I prance everywhere."

They made their way to Tito's Time Munchers French Mexican Taco Cafe and slid into seats outside the rightmost window.

"You know, as rough as this name is, I still think it beats Time Cops Kettle Pop Corn Emporium."

"So, you've been around this place? Seen a lot?"

"I've been here for about a year already."

"That's exciting. I'm clearly awed. I'm raising my menu now."

"I'll be here when you're done."

Pause.

"Are you still there?"

"I am, but I'm already done eating."

She put the menu down.

"How's the food?"

He looked at her.

"Great. But I prefer the view."

"Ugh. That was terrible." But she smiled.

"I know. I'm actually kind of ashamed. I wish time travel were possible. We could find a time machine and go back and wipe that."

Kerys paused for a second and looked at Albio. She cocked her head.

"What's your name?"

"It's Al- Albio."

"I'm forgetting that, even as we speak."

"Oh, Cleo…"

"I'm Kerys. Nice to meet you."

"Really? That's a coincidence. I named all my stuffed animals Kerys when I was younger."

"I love how that's probably true and you're actively an insane person."

"It doesn't matter. Once we find a time machine, I can erase it all."

She laughed. Albio realized that he had been holding his breath waiting for the moment he could hear her laugh again. And it was worth it.

He smiled at her.

Kerys smiled back and whispered.

"There's probably one behind this place."

Chapter Fourteen:

Bill Murphy

The time traveler's convention had one big theme. You guessed it. Time travel. Time travel movies, books, tv shows, were represented all over the place. Everywhere you looked.

From H.G. Wells, to Octavia Butler, to, well...

To other stuff not as good as that. By that, I don't mean Phillip K. Dick or Larry Niven. These are fine writers. And books. And movies.

You sometimes have to aim a bit lower.

In 2304, one of the biggest and most lucrative film franchises was born. The initial film was made by Trini Ropa, a young Jamaican college graduate who created a film that became head canon for an entire generation.

In the movie, a woman inherited a large carnival. The carnival was so massive that there was no way for her to possibly staff it. So she tried to sell it.

But no one would buy.

So she went to a friend, a psychic she had had a relationship with in college. The psychic told her she was still in love with her.

And she would help.

She used her psychic powers to pull carnival workers - clowns from all periods throughout history. And all of them became enslaved by her powers and worked on the carnival.

The first film - Time Clowns - grossed over a billion dollars. Within a year, she had written and released Time Clowns 2: Carnival Eternal.

This also did extremely well.

Less than a year later came Time Clowns 3: The infinite Big Top.

A year later, came two films - Time Clowns 4: Epiphany part 1,

and Time Clowns 4: Epiphany part 2.

You probably see where this is going. Amidst the Back to the Future tropes and Terminator cosplayers, were literally thousands of clowns.

Clowns of all kinds.

Big ones, little ones, evil ones, kind ones.

Clowns.

And Shuro Del was dressed like one.

He followed Albio and Kerys through the convention, not closely enough to be seen.

But closely enough to see.

It wasn't hard for Albio to slip the t-shirt in his winnings and give it to her.

And pulling it on her gave him the chance to unlatch the battery pack for her time vest.

Shuro Del tried to look the other way when the two of them pulled up behind this restaurant or this stand to get to know each other better. But there is only so much looking away you can do if your job is to trail people and participate.

This is the kind of thing that would have been incredibly fun with Kai around. He would have thought of every dirty joke necessary to explain what they were watching.

He would have just had fun.

And since he was gone, it had gotten harder and harder for Shuro to just let go and have fun.

Tonight, in this clown costume, traipsing after two people he knew were destined to fall in love, he was excited. He felt a little alive. And the thing about Kai is that was when his spirit was there the most. Right when everything got interesting. Right when people were really enjoying themselves.

He followed them to the X-men Days of Future Pasta bar and waited.

Here is the problem with time travel narratives. First of all, we're bouncing around in time a lot. It may be hard for you to keep track of which version of me was doing what. Even if we were wearing nametags and numbers, my convoluted narrative may have added complexities of their own.

Even if you cold see everything I do, you still might miss the bigger picture.

So, maybe a recap.

The original me was here at this convention. She's hanging out with Albio, right now, probably performing some lewd act near someone I am nearly 100% sure is actually a John Cusack. Blu and I showed up at this convention for a bit, mostly naked and surrounded by clowns, which i now realize were probably Shuro's friends trying to take care of us. Albio screwed up after collecting some Mitches and ended up here for about a year. He will send me back to the beginning with a concussion gun, wearing a t-shirt with the right temporal signature, a ruined timevest, and a rubber ball that blocks the time beacon.

Then, he goes back, without using the snapback, and gives me the concussion gun, the shirt, and a dumb note so I would meet him here, which I did, about a week-and-a-half ago. Now this version of me is going to wait until he sends old me back and causes a ruckus, a rukus we will then use to steal Bill Murphy.

I think that's it.

"So, I was gone when it happened, happens. Will happen. Anywho, when I go back what goes on?"

Reina looked at me. "This is conjecture, because, to me, it hasn't happened yet. I was not there. But you being shot and sent back without a vest on will violate safety protocols and cause a general lockdown. Now, there are people here from your timeline who MIGHT be affected by the beacon too, depending on when they left to come here. So they may panic because they will be trapped."

"So, alarms, etc."

"Yes. Alarms, lockdown, etc."

"And Albio can get back?"

"Well, on one hand, he did already. But that's not consequential, really."

The thought. "If he blinks out quickly before anyone stops him."

"But they'll be after him?"

"Yes. A lot of panic. And we can use that?"

"Anything else you want to steal, while we're at it?"

Reina looked at me. This was the moment of truth for us as friends.

"I always wanted that DeLorean from Back to the Future."

"Nice. I would have pegged you more as an H.G. Wells girl."

"It's classy, no doubt. I love the little machine with the cigar in it. I used to fantasize about that cigar going back in time and raising a whole race of little cigars."

"Oh my god. I think I did too."

We were on the other side of the rotunda now. I looked up and there it was.

Bill Murphy.

"He's a tall motherfucker." I thought, absolutely out loud.

"I hear the original Bill Murphy was twelve feet tall. They had to shoot his co-stars closer up so that they looked the same size.

I knew that wasn't true, but I looked at Reina. I hoped it was. Please let that be true.

"I hear he used to roar like a lion on set and he chewed off Chris Elliott's pinky finger."

"Fucker had it coming."

She wasn't wrong.

"Do you ever wonder what people are going to say about you hundreds of years after you're gone?"

"Yeah. But I did some things that I didn't do for a legacy. I just did them so that there were a few less unhappy people in some timeline somewhere."

"Who needs a legacy?"

"Yeah. I mean, this right here is fucked up, but…"

"Totally. They gave him buck teeth."

"And shoved a billion dollar piece of electronics up his ass."

I stole a drink from a girl walking by.

"To Bill Murphy."

She took a swig, too,

"Long may he roar."

See, this sucks too, because there is no way to say, "Meanwhile" when people who are really important to the story are waiting in a park in one century while you're trying to steal a poorly named buck-toothed statue in a different one.

But, if you can, imagine this.

There is a bald half-Asian Dutch girl sitting on the swings with a sexy dark little gnome and a big blonde teddybear right next to her. She's talking with her hands, which she does a lot.

About fifty feet away is a girl of about thirty or so, possibly Jamaican, with light skin and freckles everywhere.

And I do mean everywhere.

Her hair is wild and untamed, natural and fluid, moving with the wind. And she takes her shoes off whenever she has the chance, because she likes to feel the grass under her feet, especially when it's a tiny bit cold and wet, in the warm air.

She's one of the things that the universe seems most proud of today. It points its finger here, at her, and it says, "This. I made this.

And, man, it's really something."

And the universe isn't wrong.

And that place where that finger tapped, it brightens a bit. It's like a window to the bright daylight with a hole in it, letting in the light. It pulls her in. And the swirl of light disappears.

And she's somewhere else.

Shuro slides up beside Albio and Kerys. A flash from a device in his hand and he removes her temporal signature.

Shuro hands her a card in one hand.

And pulls his nose off, tapping it in the front and placing it in her other hand.

She laughs.

Albio picks her up and kisses her hard. Part of him hopes she can feel all of what he feels. Part of him knows she won't.

He holds her from behind and slides the battery out of her harness. He slips the shirt back over her head and she feels something.

It's hard to tell what.

Albio pulls out the concussion gun. To him, it seems to happen in slow motion. She reads the card and automatically inhales. His heart drops to the floor and he pulls the trigger.

Kerys shoots backward into the chamber and disappears.

He knew it was supposed to happen, but it looked wrong. She fell badly. What if she broke her neck? What if he killed her?

What if he fucking killed her?

He slid the gun into his bag and felt Shuro's hand drag him away. A pasty security person yells out and starts chasing.

"Run," Shuro pulls at him but Albio can't move.

What if he killed her?

The security guard tries to jump closer.

His vest doesn't work. He must be from the same timeline.

The blocker made it back.

A few people begin to yell. More vests that don't work.

Albio looks at the clown in front of him. If the blocker made it back in one piece, she probably did, too.

He started running.

Then disappeared.

And that's when we heard The alarms from the other side of the rotunda.

I don't want to make it sound like this part of the plan was difficult, because it wasn't. When everybody is running around using a time vest to travel, it's actually fairly easy to enforce rules.

To wipe your memory when you leave.

To manage your travel into and out.

To keep you from stealing important fixtures.

Easy.

But Reina and I weren't using time vests anymore. And this place wasn't ready for us.

I mean, yeah, it wasn't immediately obvious how we'd dig it up from the ground or lift it.

But the basics were under control.

We could get it out of here.

That was the important part.

Time travel is a little bit like memory. Eventually, it's hard to start placing things. Eventually, it's hard to start figuring out if the sequence of events is the one you remember.

Or if it's the real one.

I don't want to shit on causality, but eventually, we learn that time is sort of our invention. That there's a reason why the universe can so easily tolerate a cause happening after an effect, or why it's so comfortable letting things exist that had to origin in that timeline.

Because we're creating time with every breath. And maybe if we're listening, we hear it all around us.

"It doesn't matter whose idea it is. It's ours now. It doesn't matter where it came from. It's here now. "

And we have to shrug and accept it.

In that forest glenn outside peoria it was someone's idea. And I can't for the life of me remember whose.

But one of us explained how all this ends.

Not with robots killing boy scouts, although by all accounts boy scouts can be annoying.

Not with an onslaught of cookie cutter timelines where one man is so evil that by trying to eliminate him, people create a whitewater rush around a singular swelling timeline that pulls the whole universe into death.

Not with petty little men who are so petulant about losing a penny from the sale of a drug that should, in any right-thinking universe, be free.

But with compassion.

Sean would say it ends in enlightenment.

I can't explain exactly what enlightenment is.

Maybe it's that realization- the realization - that the universe pokes its finger at every once of us, rich or poor, pretty or not, young or old, with not just a small amount of pride.

Because we are all powerfully unlikely and yet here.

And maybe that is the spirit to keep in mind when trying to parse how an old white RV appeared in front of Bill Murphy, slamming into the immense statue, dislodging it.

And how a well-oiled team of young Mitchel Wagners in matching school uniforms stormed out, grabbing the statue, and lodging it onto the side window of the vehicle as Reina and I shot warning shots at the few security people who had ignored the alarms and stayed.

Reina covered me and I slipped into the open door.

And we got the hell out.

Albio felt lighter without the bag holding the concussion gun. But it also meant he was unarmed in a runaway RV full of fifteen or so identical delinquents.

He made his way to the front of the RV.

"Hey, man."

"What the fuck?" Bitch Mitch was driving. He was about sixteen-years-old and was definitely missing some skin on his face from the duct tape. "How the fuck did you get here?"

"Do you remember me?"

Another Mitch spoke up. "You kidnapped us."

"How are you here?"

"I stole you away from a place that was run by evil bastards. You get that, right?"

"I'M evil, Justin Beiber." He looked back. "I'm fucking evil."

"And yet, you missed running over anyone. I've driven this thing. It takes an act of god not to run over someone."

"What if I do it now?"

"You won't. You're a shitty driver, but despite all the shit they made you do, you don't really want to kill anyone."

Bitch Mitch pulled the RV over to the side of the road.

"What the fuck do YOU know?"

"A lot, actually. I just came from the future."

"Bullshit."

"Are you a reader?" Albio tossed a newspaper clipping into his lap.

"What is this?"

"Read it."

And he did. He read about a future where he raped a woman, causing a nuclear conflagration. Billions of people died.

And he spit on it.

"Here's your paper, man. Shove it up your ass."

"Do any of the rest of you want to read it."

Albio passed it around. Mitches grumbled.

"How about you, buddy?" Albio spoke to the youngest one. Nine-year-old Mitch shot back, "No. This isn't right."

Albio looked at Bitch Mitch, "It's not right, is it?"

"Fuck you, man. What do you want? What do you think you can do?"

"Tell me this. Where are you driving?"

Nine-year-old Mitch spoke up. He looked around, "We don't know."

"What if I gave you a place to go?"

Davi stepped through the light into a clearing. She could see a series of buildings in the distance. She stepped forward and slipped off her shoes. She smiled, realizing where she was.

She heard a woman's voice behind her and looked up, momentarily blinded by the sun.

"I'm glad you remember. This is where we had the idea."

The woman slid off her shoes and sat down next to her.

Davi laughed.

"What? Do I look old?"

"No way. You look good. I know black don't crack."

"I appreciate that."

"What idea?" Davi asked.

Across from her, dipping her feet in the pond, was another version of Davi.

Let's call her Davina.

Davina was possibly forty-five. Maybe fifty.

With her it was hard to tell.

Davina took the younger woman's hand.

"To teach them, not kill them. To take however long it takes and teach them."

"That was my idea?"

"I think so. So long ago."

"And you're me?"

"Oh, no. I'm you from a different timeline. I got here later. We don't age here."

"It's a loop."

"It's a ground. Come on. I'll show you around."

Davina took Davi's hand and they walked toward the buildings.

To their left was the boy scout camp where a version of Mitchel Wagner was murdered.

They passed a white RV. It looked a little more worn than last she saw it.

"That thing still runs, actually."

"No way. It barely ran back then."

"Well, it's not aging anymore."

"And we don't, either?"

"No. And neither do they." She pointed to the group of kids playing. "They stay here until they're ready."

"No matter how long it takes?"

"Yep."

Davina and Davi stopped at the foot of a very large statue.

Davi cocked her head, "Who is Bill Murphy?"

Davina laughed. "I don't think that's important. The statue is the ground. It's what keeps us in a constant time loop."

"Come on, I'll introduce you to the kids."

"I think I met the Mitchels."

"Oh, that's just a small part now. Let's just say that this has kind of caught on. This is where they bring the bad ones now. And we treat them like they aren't."

"And it works?"

"Eventually, yes."

Davi stopped. "I can't. This sounds... I mean. What about Sean? What about Kerys?"

"He'll be here. They'll all be here. That's the thing about what we do."

"What do you mean, 'what we do'?'"

"When you can be anywhere, you go where you choose. Do you believe that Sean will choose to be with you? And the rest?"

"I do."

"I learned a long time ago to love like this," she opened her hand and showed her palm, "And not like this," She closed her hand into a fist.

"I like that." she put her hand in Davina's.

"I'll go for the tour."

And I did go. We all did. After all, we needed a place to put the people who were truly horrible, somewhere that had the time it took to make a difference.

Ten-thousand years.

Ten-thousand things.

Whichever comes first.

In this timeline, we don't use vests anymore. And we know the dangers of trying to build cookie cutter timelines. Diversity across the timestream is our goal. We try to maximize happiness. And we never changed our motto.

Because Fuck Cancer.

But we work with a more delicate hand now.

And we watch the lights endemic to the universe around us.

And listen hard to hear what it has to say.

Even if it sounds a little crazy at first.

Futtitysnob.

KETAMINE RUSH

Epilogue: The Clown Rule

They found Arnold J. Marasco at his nephew's birthday party, in Joliet, Illinois. They had been looking for this version, the sunburned one that knew exactly what he was doing. The one who traveled to the apocalypse and thought, "Yes, this, I will make this unstoppable."

The one who wanted to see everything burn.

You see, not all Arnold J. Marasco's were like this. Not all of them were businessmen without a sense of justice or humanity. There was one, in this timeline here, who became a lawyer to help the disenfranchised, people who would otherwise have gone unrepresented.

There was one, in this timeline, who created a tool that helped people with dementia, and he priced it so low that it was available easily. And for those who couldn't pay, it was free. Was he a great man? Maybe not. But not an evil one.

Shuro Del was in full clown costume. At his side, Reina wore just a black sundress as she drank in the summer sun. The children scattered as they marched toward the ruddy Marasco, drinking at a picnic table.

Another Marasco stepped out from the kitchen, light gun in his hand. "There are ten more of me in the trees around us. Are you sure this is something you want to do?"

Shuro threw his vest down in front of him. there was a symbol of a hand in it, something Albio had fished out of that room at EntheoGen.

Arnold J. Marasco remembered. After a little prodding.

He'd have time.

Epilogue: Floating in the river.

And so I travel with Albio a lot now.

He makes it easy.

And we bring things and do things and live through things. We don't need sex to travel, but sometimes we do it anyway. I don't need it, but I do it. The swirls of light are a part of us now, and they aren't about need as much as they are about pointing out something the universe thinks is pretty special. Like pins in the map of everything. I realize now, when I look at him, that he is a pinhole where the universe stuck a pin. There, this place. This is where it's worth being. This is special. This is who we are and this is where we travel.

And the light spills out of him.

And there are others. And we travel there.

And I travel sometimes with Blu too. And I let myself go, trying to see how far we can get and what can happen next. And she likes to be naked now, and I like it when she is, too. She accepts being loved so well now that I'm reminded that all that shit is a skill you can exercise.

You can learn it.

And I would keep a diary of her because she is fascinating, but no one would ever believe it. Sometimes she even has hair. But that only lasts until she gets sick of it and cuts it all off again.

I've run out of bald jokes about twenty times, but she pretends they're all new again.

And sometimes Los is there, usually quiet, but he opens up more when we're alone. He sang to me once while we were floating naked in a pool four-thousand years ago and his voice was not bad. I closed my eyes and let myself fall in love. We had sex in the water and both thought there were definitely better places to do that.

So we found better ones.

And sometimes I travel with other people, because once you see the light in someone, it makes it harder to miss it in someone else. I don't miss it anymore when I see it. Not everyone is a good travel partner, but there are so many worlds out there, it's worth it to just try.

People are worth it.

And I find myself back in Albio's arms a lot, telling him all about it, or listening to him, or just exploring and reminding myself that time is full of reasons, some subtle and some huge, to wait for the next minute to come, not with anxiousness or dread, but with maybe a little wonder at what is about to happen next. He is a great example of that.

We visit Sean sometimes at his free clinic. It took him about a year to reverse engineer those pills, so we don't need to bring him boxes anymore. He gets to see people find themselves every day, and it's where he wants to be. And sometimes his brother works with him and he loves that. They do interviews and tell magazines that the universe invented it.

Because the universe wants people to share in their own creation and shine.

He tries to get home to Davina as often as he can. About ten different versions of her now work at her school for the infinite, in an eternal loop, working with and training people who might have done horrible things without her. She's always there if I want to dance with her or whisper together. There are older versions of her and younger versions, and I love them all.

My favorite version is always the one I'm with.

And I know the universe has to birth some bad things along with the good. I know that oranges are born alongside hurricanes. But hating the bad seems pointless when you can spend your time building the good. Sure, the universe isn't perfect. But perfection is something that happens in people's eyes, not on their faces.

We're all flawed. And we're worth loving.

Why not a flawed universe?

KETAMINE RUSH